I0624744

S. A. ROWLAND

Water to Water

A Collection of Short Stories

First published by Water to Water Publishing 2023

Copyright © 2023 by S. A. Rowland

First edition

ISBN: 979-8-218-29674-2

Editing by Leya Booth
Cover art by Nejc Planinšek

This book was professionally typeset on Reedsy.
Find out more at reedsy.com

Contents

Sea Glass

Raindrops patter against my windshield. With a squeal, the wiper interrupts the rhythmic pattern. My view is clear for a few moments before the rain reclaims the glass. The road in front of me twists and curves like a serpent, cutting through a wall of tall evergreens and the darkness beyond. It has rained my entire drive, but it suits my mood. I let myself fade to the sound of the heavy rain landing on the exterior of my car. It's so easy to fade into my surroundings now that I am alone. This is my form of self-preservation.

But I should let guilt drench my bones. I deserve far worse. I extinguished the light of my world and now I must live in the darkness. I killed my wife. I killed the person I cared about the most. It wasn't intentional. I dreamed that she would live forever by my side. I believed we were invincible. Untouchable to the decaying world. In careless glee, I risked her life and lost.

That night, I drank too much. I shouldn't have gotten behind the wheel and she shouldn't have gotten into the passenger seat. With confidence, I assured her that I could get us home. And I've paid for the words ever since. I've paid for them legally, but it's not enough. I need to die too. My death would even the scales of my consciousness and in death, we could be together again.

The sea glass in the passenger seat clinks and clatters in its bucket as I round each curve. Soft blues, greens, browns, and clear pieces of glass gather in the same bucket. I have amassed dozens of pieces in various sizes and shapes. Beautiful to look at and surely enough to grant my wish.

My grandmother told me stories of a specific beach near my childhood home where mermaids lived. Beautiful women with long drenched locks and fish-like tails frolic in the waves there. Mischievous creatures, my grandmother warned me that the mermaids were sometimes responsible for dragging lone swimmers down to their deaths. But my grandmother also told me that if I was ever in need, those creatures can grant wishes for the right price. They don't care for money or jewels, but they do have an affinity for sea glass. With the bucket next to me, I will wish to be reunited with my dead wife. I will gladly spend my entirety in the underworld as long as she remains by my side. I would wander through Limbo smiling as long as her hand was interlocked with mine. Even if my gift displeases them and they choose to drown me, I will search tirelessly for my wife on the other side. I will hold her close and beg for her forgiveness.

After hours on the road, I finally arrive at the beach and park. I walk over the tall dunes and the endless ocean fills my vision. The dark blue water reflects the moon's illumination. The surface seems still, but the waves regularly crash upon the shore. It looks like I am the only creature on this beach, but I know there are mermaids under the water's surface.

I walk across the sand and directly into the waves, letting the water soak my shoes and trousers. I won't need them anymore. I gently shake my bucket of sea glass and wait for a response. The water remains still.

"I have a gift," I shout into the ocean. "I have many pieces of sea glass that I would like to trade for a wish."

I walk deeper into the water. It reaches my chest now.

"I would like to ask for a wish, please," desperation seeps into my voice. I think of seeing my wife again and I can't help but sob. Salty tears flow down my cheeks and mix with the saltwater ocean. There is a splash to my left and my heart lifts. The silhouette of a head emerges from the water.

"Let me see that," a silky voice asks before pulling the bucket from my hands. She runs her fingers across the pieces of glass, savoring their gentle clinking, before asking, "What is it you want?"

"I want to be with my wife. She was everything to me, but she is dead."

A second mermaid emerges from the dark sea. She takes the bucket under the waves with her.

"You want to be with your dead wife?" the first mermaid confirms.

"Yes, I want nothing more."

"Then consider your trade accepted and your wish granted."

Sliding behind me, she wraps her arms around my torso and begins pulling me deeper into the wave. I don't resist. She is as gentle as the tides. The mermaid drags me under the surface. Deeper and deeper she pulls me. Soon, the water is jet black and the light from the moon is no longer visible. My lungs are burning, but I focus on the pressure of her body on my back to try to drown out the pain. And then, my consciousness fades to black.

I wake up with sand crusting my face. My throat is sore and scratchy and my body feels dusty. I sit up and notice the sun sitting on the ocean's horizon. In despair, I realize that I am alive. I jump up to throw myself back into the ocean, but then I see a form lying next to me. Her small frame is curled into a fetal position. I rush to her side and brush back her hair from her face.

Joy strikes my heart like lightning. It is my wife's face hiding under thick brown hair. Her gentle breaths disrupt the sand she sleeps upon. My beautiful wife, the light of my world, lays sleeping before me. We are reunited, but I didn't have to die for us to be together again. The mermaid misinterpreted my wish in the best possible way.

But before the guilt can evaporate, I need to ask my wife a question. One that I prepared to ask in my death but instead now have the opportunity to ask in life. I pull her towards my lap and gently shake her shoulder until her eyelashes flutter open.

"Hazel, I need to know, do you forgive me?"

She stares deeply into my eyes and places her hand upon my arm before uttering, "Of course I do."

Relief washes over me. We are together and nothing will part us again.

I lift her into my arms as I stand. "Let's go home."

Melody

To generations of children in this small town, I have been branded a witch. In whispered voices, they tell each other of my supposed misdeeds. Of the multitudes of small boys and girls that I have lured to my cottage and eaten. Of the potions I have sold to women hoping to get rid of their husbands. Of the father I have killed.

The braver children will ride their bikes down the road to my mailbox. They will point up my gravel driveway, past my small pond, to my cottage. Arms outstretched, they dare their friends to get closer. They dare each other to leave the security of the pavement and take their chances with the witch.

The bravest child is Kevin. Kevin will stroll five steps onto my property. He will turn to his friends and call them cowards. Sometimes he will even saunter up to my pond. Staring deeply into the water, he will claim that he sees the eyes of murdered children.

I understand why they think I'm a witch. As an older woman living alone, it comes with the territory. I've let my gray hair grow down to my legs. My baggy clothes lay loose on my body. With no one else around, why dress up?

As soon as the creaking of my screen door reaches their ears, they grab their bikes. They disperse faster than cockroaches when the light flips on. And I am alone again.

The adults of this small town have branded me a hermit. The boogeymen of their childhood have no weight in their adult world. They have an explanation for everything.

"Melody had a rough childhood that caused her to hide from the world," one would say and the others would nod in agreement.

"Poor thing, to have her mother run off and for her father to pass away like that," someone else would add.

A bunch of lousy gossips they all are. To pity me because my father died? He is better off dead, the bastard. My father was an aggressive man. He demanded to be served like he believed a man should. My poor mother couldn't meet all his demands while raising a small child. She would flit through the house. She would move between stirring a pot on the stove, returning a discarded item, washing a dish, and back to the stove. Like a hummingbird, she couldn't stop moving. If she did, my father was on her.

He would only speak to her with complaints. Something was always wrong. She would apologize with her eyes as wide as headlights. If he was sober, that would be it. If he had been drinking, she wasn't so lucky. When my mother was alive, it seemed like she was always sporting a bruise. The first lesson my mother taught me was to fear my father.

Then one day it was different. I was only six when my father stepped on the colored pencils I left on the floor. He screamed at my mother for not cleaning up after her spawn. Instead of her usual apology, she silently stood up, her face flat and emotionless, and walked out the door. My father's face was enraged. He grimaced in anger, slamming the door as he followed her out. I covered my ears to muffle the sound of his voice. I hid under the table and waited.

Minutes later, he returned. His pants were soaked and he was dripping water onto the floor.

"GET OUT FROM THERE!" he bellowed. "Your mother has run off. Now it's up to you, Melody, to make dinner. And clean up this water." He slammed his hand on the table to emphasize his order.

He told everyone in town who would listen that my mother ran off with another man. They cooed sympathetically and cursed her name.

For the next eight years, I filled the hole my mother left. I ensured that dinner was on the table at six-thirty sharp. The dishes were washed, dried, and put away before I went to bed. Coffee and breakfast were ready at seven in the morning with a packed lunch beside it. Floors were swept and mopped each afternoon. The laundry hung to dry each Saturday. It was exhausting.

5

Our routine lasted until the night my father died. That particular night, he followed me into my bed for the first and only time. His hand covered my mouth, but I knew better than to scream. He fell into a deep sleep after he was done using me.

I waited until his breaths were even before I slipped out of the bed. Silently, I crept from my home and gently closed the door behind me. The wet grass kissed my bare feet. A full moon reflected from the pond and drew me nearer.

I didn't let myself cry in front of my father. I couldn't bear to show weakness to him. But now the tears streamed down my face. As they fell into the pond, small ripples interrupted the moon's reflection.

"Melody, you are hurting," a small voice whispered from the pond, "but you do not deserve it. I can offer you a solution. I can end your pain." The moon's reflection rippled.

"How?" I asked, wiping my face on my sleeve.

"I can offer you a gift. The ability to kill whomever you touch. You could kill your father with a small brush of your fingers. His heart will stop in an instant."

I hesitated, "But what do you want from me?"

"I will expect nothing from you for the next fifty years."

"But what will you expect from me in fifty years?"

"I will expect you to make a choice. That is all."

I pondered the offer. I wouldn't have to serve him anymore. No one would fill my body with dread. I could say what I wanted and do as I pleased. Life without my father would be far easier. I could live for myself and no one else. I would be free. And in fifty years, I would be an old woman. There is not much a sixty-four-year-old woman can do anyway.

"I accept."

The ripples through the pond became larger.

"Then it is done," the voice spoke for the last time.

The ripples sank into the pond. The tension around me dissipated. Insects that were silent before began to sing.

I sat at the table until morning. When it was time, I made my father's breakfast and coffee. I placed two slices of buttered toast and two fried eggs on a plate. I centered his plate in front of his chair. Then I waited at the table. He finally awoke to sit in front of his meal. Before he could grab his fork, I gave his hand a squeeze. My father looked up to meet my gaze. My eyes burned with hatred. Then his shoulders slumped down and his face fell into his plate. I was filled with elation.

After my father's departure, I built my home inside of our old house. I added shelves to fill with books. The smell of baked bread, cakes, and cookies permeated through the space. A curled cat would keep my chair warm. I placed vases with flowers in every room. My garden displayed a variety of flowers within a lush green backdrop. There were splashes of yellows, blues, pinks, purples, and whites. I felt so much delight in my home. I didn't spend much time out of it and that was for the best. I never wanted to touch another person again.

I wouldn't say that I am a bad person for killing my father. I never felt guilty for doing it. Some people deserve death.

Most people don't deserve an early departure. Most people are trying to get by with the cards they were dealt and I cannot be a judge or an executioner. So it is best that I live alone.

I have enough property to grow plenty of food. Wheat, corn, potatoes, tomatoes, cucumbers, squash, and more grow in neat lines. I had the foresight to plant apple and peach trees many years ago. No matter how much I feast in the summer and fall, I always have enough to can and save for the winter. My deadly gift only seems to apply to people and I am thankful for that.

For pocket change, I have a local woman that comes by once a week. I leave a basket of fresh-cut flowers and baked goods by the door. She sells these in town, takes her cut of the money, and leaves the rest in a basket by my door. It has been a good arrangement.

The money has been useful for new clothes when needed, or various foodstuffs when desired. But most of the money goes towards books. Because of the books, my life spent in this home has felt fulfilling. I can read of people, places, and experiences that I will never know.

It's almost unfortunate how good stories can draw you into a world so unlike your own. You grow so attached to the characters and so thrilled by the adventure that when it ends, a hole is left in your heart. Finishing a good story can create an emptiness. But coming back to it later is how I imagine meeting an old friend is like, warm and comforting, like home.

Fifty years spent in this comfort passed faster than I expected. I didn't know it was time until Kevin went into the pond. Like many sunny Saturdays before it, this warm day brings the children to my mailbox. Their brave leader strolls past the others. Young Kevin walks to the edge of the pond. Then he leans forward and pretends to listen to the pond.

Kevin turns to his friends and shouts, "Gracey, it says that you're next."

Kevin unleashes an impish smile as Gracey shakes her head and steps further back. But then his smile sinks and is replaced with a look of horror. Kevin turns to look at the pond, but misplaces his footing and falls in. His body flails in the water. Kevin's 'arms splash helplessly, but he can't find anything to hold on to.

"He can't swim," a child shouts from my mailbox.

I run from my home and beg the children to help him. I entreat them to reach into the pond and pull him out.

"She's trying to kill all of us too!" one screams.

"The witch wants to murder us all!" another responds.

They quickly hop onto their bikes and speed off.

I make it to the edge of the pond, where Kevin has stopped chopping the water. He has sunk to the bottom. It has only been a few moments since he has gone under. There is still a good chance he can be saved. But what good can I do? If I try to save Kevin from drowning, I may kill him with my touch.

I am lost. What should I do? What can I do? Tears wet my face for the first time in fifty years. I take a deep breath and step into the pond. Reaching around the dark bottom, I find Kevin's thin arm. It is cold and feels delicate in my hands. I worry that a hard tug would break it.

I gently pull Kevin to the surface. I place his small body upon the grass. Hovering with my ear above his mouth, I can't hear any breath entering or leaving his body. His stomach doesn't rise or fall. Moving my ear to his chest, no drumbeat greets me. Kevin is dead.

Sitting in the grass, I sob. I don't know if I killed Kevin or I let him die.

8

Either way, Kevin's death is squarely on my shoulders.

Soon I hear cars coming down the road, but my attention is fixated on Kevin. His wet hair is plastered along his face. He looks so cold. No one can mistake him for a sleeper. No one sleeps drenched and freezing like that.

"He fell into the pond and couldn't swim," I tell the first person that approaches.

The man merely nods. More cars arrive. It feels crowded, which is not a good feeling for someone who kills at the slightest touch.

I retreat into my home and watch the scene unfolding from my window. Partially hidden behind my curtain, I watch as more people arrive. There are gestures at my cottage. Eventually, an officer knocks on my door. I replay the events to the officer, without mentioning my condition. He takes some notes and leaves satisfied.

I return to the window and catch the gaze of a man. He watches my home without moving. His square shoulders and untrimmed stubble give him a jagged look. The anger that sits on his face only makes him look more gruesome. His face tells me everything. He knows that I am responsible for the death of his son. There will be no forgiveness. The violence in his stare sends shivers down my spine.

The day wanes and people trickle back home. I make sure to lock my doors that night because I can still feel that man's hatred. Glancing out my window, I see the moon's reflection in my pond. As I watch the moon, I hear a truck approaching. After a few moments, the truck comes into view. It meanders up my driveway and parks in front of my cottage. This man intends to kill me and I can't blame him. Because of me, his son didn't come home.

A shotgun-toting silhouette steps from the truck and approaches my front door. My heart beats throughout my body. I silence the cries making their way up my throat. I run into my bedroom and into my closet. Pulling my closet door closed, I hear him kicking. My wooden door splinters under his force. My heartbeat is only in my ears now.

I can stop him. One touch and he would fall to the ground. I could live another day. But could I forget the hatred in his eyes? Could I forget Kevin's cold body? So full of childish glee one moment, but so empty the next. My head swims. What should I do?

I can hear the man moving through my house now. He is getting close, but what choice do I make?

Changeling

The photo from the flier captures my attention. I've seen this photo several times, but I continue to find my gaze landing on her. Based on the photo, I imagine that Grace was a friendly person. She smiled with her entire face, from her perfect teeth to her large brown eyes. Her eyes were a shade of brown so dark that the iris and the pupil were indistinguishable. Freckles dusted the bridge of Grace's nose, and strawberry blonde hair tumbled down her back. The woman in the photo was beautiful and exuded liveliness. The photo contrasted heavily with the rest of the flier.

Grace Patterson
20 Years Old
Missing since September 18th
Last Seen Leaving Harrill Hall at Western Carolina University in Cullowhee, NC
Anchor tattoo on left wrist

It's been over two months and we have nothing. Nothing has changed since her parents came to us, begging us to bring their baby girl home. It is not through lack of trying. We've all put so much effort into this investigation. I've talked to each family member, friend, and ex. I've pulled phone records and tracked her bank cards. I've read through weeks of messages across her social media accounts. I've grabbed transit records for everything leaving this town. Her parents have even put together a large reward for anyone who can help bring Grace home. Regardless, no tips have come forward. There hasn't been any trace of Grace since September 18th.

Several of Grace's friends worry that Grace killed herself. Grace had recently been dumped by her high school sweetheart during a house party. Many people came forward saying that she left the party with her face stained with tears and mascara. A few days later, Grace told her roommate that she felt the water calling to her. Grace thought that the cold water of a nearby stream would soothe the pain in her heart. I didn't like the idea that Grace would commit suicide. A young woman so full of life couldn't have been cut down in her prime by an immature boy like that.

But I couldn't leave any stone unturned. We dredged the nearby waterways and found nothing. I reached out to forensics experts. They would dump dummies with trackers into the streams and rivers at various points. Each weighed over 100 pounds and resembled a crash test dummy. Well, they were practically crash test dummies. Supposedly these dummies would act like a human body as it tumbled through the water. Our expert would see where the dummies got caught on rocks and logs and where they finally landed on shore. No dummy made it more than a few miles. We visited every stick, rock, and shoreline that the expert marked and there was nothing. Not even a scrap of Grace's clothing. It was another dead end.

I've caught myself staring into her face from the flier. I have hope that she is still out there, because I can't imagine her dead. Grace is young, effervescent, vigorous, and beautiful. She is so very beautiful. I recognize that I have never met her, so I would call my feelings complicated. I guess that I don't even know how to describe my feelings for Grace.

These feelings for Grace started a week after she went missing. At that point, many still had hope that Grace was alive. For the first days of my investigation, this was just another missing persons case. Tragic and unfortunate, but it didn't hit home for me.

My change in perspective came when Grace visited me. Whether this visit took place in a dream or reality, I couldn't tell you. Perhaps Grace met me somewhere between asleep and awake. Regardless, I felt her slip under the sheets next to me. The warmth of her body pressed against mine. Her soft hair nuzzled against my chest and under my chin. Her hair smelled like strawberries.

Her presence caused my heartbeat to quicken. There was electricity running through my veins. I felt a desire deeper and stronger than I've ever known before. I kissed the top of her head, rubbed my face over her smooth hair. Lifting her chin and lowering my face, I brought my lips to her lips. The electricity passed back and forth between us. It was like how the waves pass back and forth between the shore and the ocean. Her kisses were gentle at first, but the swell of our passion grew.

I ran my hands through her hair, down her back, over her breasts to finally grip her thighs. Each new texture and shape was a delight. Between kisses, I pulled off her clothes. My excitement grew the further we went and I could not stop until I reached completion. I brought my lips to her neck, savoring her soft moans and the way she kicked her feet and curled her toes. I moved down, massaging, kissing, sucking, licking her breasts. Continuing downward, I placed slow kisses on the inside of her thigh. I alternated kissing each thigh until her hands held my head in place. I took pleasure in the sharp breaths and soft moans that escaped her lips. Her knees shifted and then stiffened. The toes on each of her feet squeezed together and her breathing stopped for a few moments.

After Grace caught her breath, I brought my face to hers. Her right hand wrapped around my neck and her left hand grabbed my wrist. I watched as her anchor tattoo moved from her arm to mine. With a warm tingling sensation, the anchor drifted down my arm, around my chest, and settled on my back.

Grace brought my mouth to hers and in the same motion I slipped myself inside of her. We made love slowly, continually exchanging kisses and caresses. I shifted her weight to pull her on top of me. Moonlight slipped through the window. It cast a pale glow across her soft stomach and round breasts. She smiled and my heart melted. I was in love. Grace leaned down and I pulled her closer. My mouth never left hers as I finished inside of her.

Grace grabbed my left wrist again to take her tattoo back. She smiled widely, like in her flier, before withdrawing herself from me. Repositioning herself, she laid her head on my shoulder. She pressed the length of her naked form against mine. Exhausted, we both fell asleep.

When I woke up the next morning, I was alone. Regardless, I could not stop thinking of Grace. My thoughts were drawn to her and the memories of our night together retained an electric quality. Nothing in my life could compare to our wonderful time together.

Everything now is pointless without her. Each day is bland because I am incomplete without Grace. I cannot be whole again until I find her and hold her again. I stare at her flier and think about the day I can bring her home. I think of a lifetime of her body shifting under mine.

Days turn into weeks with only a memory to sustain me. I fear the worst when the call finally comes. I imagine her decomposing body hidden under a pile of freshly fallen leaves in the woods. I imagine her drenched hair splattered across what remained of her smile as she washed up on shore. I imagined the worst, but she is alive. She is alive and I wasn't the one to find her.

Grace was found walking back and forth along a bridge, over a river we searched many times. Confused, she had no recollection of who she was, why she was there, how she got there, or where she was.

Medical testing reveals that she is perfectly healthy. There are no signs of trauma to explain the amnesia. Additionally, nothing is found in her bloodwork. We don't find a single substance to explain her memory loss. Even though Grace was found in a relatively remote area, she is still a healthy weight. Nothing suggests she spent months braving the elements and brisk seasonal temperatures.

With medical tests in hand, we worry Grace was kidnapped. But we don't know if she escaped or if she was released. Either way, there is a possibility that a kidnapper is still at large. We bring in a psychologist to work with Grace. We all hope the right line of questions will glean some insight into her ordeal. And Grace has provided us with many questions to draw from.

I had to pull a lot of strings to work directly with the psychologist, but it is worth it to finally be in the same room as Grace. I hope that she will recognize me from our night together. Even if it was a dream, it was a dream we both had to have shared.

Seated next to the psychologist, I ensure that I keep my emotions under check. But when Grace enters the room, I know something is wrong. I can't explain it, but as soon as I see her, my heart drops in disappointment. She is flat and lacks the electricity I remember.

The psychologist's questions yield nothing. Grace still can't tell us who she is, let alone where she has been. She tells us that her parents are treating her well, but she can't replicate their feelings. To her, they are still strangers. We all are strangers to Grace.

When she speaks, she does not smile. Yet I wouldn't say that she is sad. Her face is like a mask that is incapable of emotion. My heart is broken. This is not the woman from the missing person flier. This is not Grace. This is not the woman who filled my head and my heart for weeks. This is not the woman who made everything else in my life dull in comparison. The woman before me is dull. Superficially, the features of Grace and this woman match. But I know in my bones that the woman before me is an imposter.

Once I accept this as truth, my eyes are drawn to the characteristics that are wrong. Grace's skin was perfect ivory. Her freckles dotted her face like the constellations that dotted the night sky. The imposter's skin is fleshy, pockmarked, and without adornment. Grace's eyes resembled melted chocolate. The imposter's eyes resemble a murky pond. More upsetting is the absence of the anchor tattoo on her wrist. A tattoo can't disappear. The real Grace took her tattoo back, so where is the tattoo now? This woman isn't Grace. But who is this imposter? And where is the real Grace?

A few nights later, I dream of vines wrapping around me. My arms and my legs are pinned down as the vines wrap tighter and tighter around my throat. Breathing becomes difficult as my neck is squeezed. I gasp for air, but nothing can get past the blockage. Lights flash at the corners of my eyesight before being replaced with blackness.

I awake gasping for air. Grabbing at my throat, I try to remove the nonexistent vines. Once my heart rate and respiration return to normal, I am able to think about my dream. I conclude that the dream was trying to tell me that the imposter is dangerous. I need to save the real Grace while there is still time.

In the daylight, I pay the imposter and Grace's family a visit. Grace's mother waves me into her home which opens into the living room. School photos of Grace and shots from family vacations are hung above the couch. Grace's parents sit on their couch while the imposter and I sit in the matching chairs that flank the couch. A coffee table separates us.

Sitting in her home makes me feel closer to Grace. I can almost pick out her scent from the surroundings. Closing my eyes, I can almost feel her arms wrapping around me. Opening my eyes cuts my fantasy short as heavy reality slaps my face.

Grace's parents do not seem to find anything wrong with the changeling that sits in their living room.

"We're so happy Grace is home," they beam. "The therapy is going so well."

I look at the fake Grace. "Is it going well?"

A small smile crosses the imposter's face. It lacks the warmth of the real Grace's smile. "Yes, my parents have helped me remember so much."

Grace's mother nods in agreement, "We've been going through our photo albums together." She points at a large book on the coffee table.

"It has been helpful," chimes fake Grace.

I lean forward. "What do you remember?"

"The memories from the album are coming back." The changeling turns to Grace's mother. "My parents have been such a great help."

The duped parents smile and nod. They have let their desperation blind them to reality. This imposter has stepped into Grace's life and they are enabling it! The fake is studying Grace's photos to better fit into the hole Grace left.

"What do you remember about your disappearance?" I ask.

"Nothing, except for feeling cool water on my face."

I thank the family for their time and I make sure that they have my number. As I leave, I promise to return later. I am frustrated with the obtuse blindness of Grace's parents. I decide to drive to the bridge where the imposter was found. I hope that the real Grace won't be far. I've walked along this bridge, road, and shoreline several times. This area is desolate. The road and the bridge cut through the remote wilderness. There are no other signs of human life.

Scrabbling down the bank, I climb to the water. I spend the next hour walking along the river. The sound of water bubbling over the rocks brings a sense of peace. Over the river, I can hear bird songs and the occasional reckless scampering of squirrels. My own steps bring the sound of crunching leaves underfoot. Despite the golden sunlight pressing through the trees, the day is cold. A gentle breeze brushes against my face like a soft palm and I smell it. I smell her. I recognize Grace's fragrance from her home.

The wind pulls me to the right, plunging into the woods. I can almost feel Grace's hand in mine, pulling me toward her. I follow with vigor. Time fades away as we walk deeper and deeper into the forest. The light begins to thin as the sun slides into the horizon. But my patience is rewarded as I see Grace standing in a clearing ahead of me. Her back is turned to me, but I know that this is the real Grace. Beautiful, lively Grace.

My heart thumps through my chest. Desire fills my veins. I run towards Grace and the earth sinks beneath my feet. Unprepared, I splash into the water. What I thought was a clearing is actually a pond. I catch my bearings and force my head past the surface. Wildly I turn, looking for Grace. The last beams of light skim the surface of the pond. My heart begins to drop into my stomach when something brushes against my leg.

Taking a deep breath, I plunge under the pond's surface. I can't see anything through the murky water, but a hand grasps mine. I follow the hand to an arm, a shoulder, and a torso. Rocks lay on top of the torso, but adrenaline gives me the strength to roll them off of the body with ease. I stand upright and pull the body with me. Clutching her to my chest, I finally feel complete. I have at last found my beautiful Grace.

The Quarry

It was a summer day so perfect that you would dream of it in the dead of winter. When the cold air scratched your face, you would think of this sun. Hanging high in the sky, the sun showered the world in dry heat. An occasional cool breeze supplied enough relief to ensure that I didn't melt into a puddle of sweat. On perfect summer days like this, I go to the quarry.

The quarry lies in a swath of nearby woods. After a short hike, these woods open up to reveal the massive pit of the quarry. This pit was created decades ago to supply materials for the nearby interstate. But over the years, rainwater filled this pit.

I'm not sure if it's because of the rain or because of the depth, but the water is crystal clear. At the edge of the quarry, you can still see your feet under you. Walking deeper into the quarry unveils the drop-off. At the drop-off, darkness lies beyond your toes. The drop-off reminds you that this is a massive pit. Even with beautiful, unclouded water like this, the light can't penetrate to such a depth. Some may worry about what lies at the bottom, hidden by the shadows. But I wouldn't fear anything you could find at the bottom of a quarry.

If the clear water surrounded by lush trees doesn't offer enough to lure people to the quarry, the cliff might. At fourteen feet high, it allows thrill-seekers to display their courage. On days like this, dozens of individuals will take their chance with this cliff. With a running start, they soar over the edge into the quarry's water below.

It's important not to second-guess yourself once you get started. The rocks along the bottom await anyone who doesn't leap far enough out. But unknown to each jumper, with each press off the cliff, the cliff erodes a little bit more. If we're being honest, that is actually a little project of mine. I've been making sure that the cliff keeps getting weaker and moving further back. The next jump will always be riskier and will need more force to clear.

You may not understand my hobbies, but I love to see hubris land on the rocks below. Like Icarus, they tried flying too close to the sun and were rewarded with a fall to the earth. No deaths yet, but the satisfying crunch of breaking bones has been enough for me so far.

To my reader, I have already revealed my true self. What can I say? I love to see others in pain. I've been around for too many lifetimes at this point and I've spent all of it inflicting suffering. And I'm not alone on this Earth. As the old saying goes, I am many. The many like me all serve the same purpose, but our methods vary. Some prefer to create emotional torture and psychological anguish. They work by whispering thoughts and scattering temptations. They slowly build their way to destruction.

I do admire those whose efforts are limited to the mind. I would even say it's art in its own form. But it takes so much time and there is so little blood. Inflicting emotional pain upon humans isn't my style. It doesn't match the satisfaction that physical torment brings. I am happy to tempt a drunkard to drink a little bit more, but only if the outcome is gory.

Sitting at the edge of the quarry, in perfect view of the cliff, I wait. Groups trickle in and select spaces around the water to set up their hammocks. Stowing coolers and bags, they stake their temporary claims of patches of earth. It isn't long before a group of girls claim the trees behind me. They drag a variety of brightly colored inflatables into the quarry with them. Soon they are giggling and splashing each other like they're a fucking advertisement. I choose to ignore them.

Now, the thrill-seekers and fools arrive to hurl themselves off the cliff. The first few sail over the rocks with ease. They splash effortlessly into the water. As expected, the first ones to make the leap are confident and sober. But given enough time, someone will slip up.

I continue to focus my attention on the cliff and my patience is rewarded. A full-bodied brunette approaches the precipice. Throwing back the last few sips of her beer, she walks backward from the edge. After pausing to drop her can, she runs forward but fumbles the last step. Her foot never pushes off the edge. Instead of gracefully leaping through the sky, she is pulled down the cliffside. I hear the crunch of broken bones followed by screams. Her anguish bounces and echoes across the quarry. It's perfect.

"That's rough dude," a voice as smooth as honey interrupts my show. "That's why you will never catch me on those cliffs."

I turn around to see a young woman standing behind me. I'm caught off guard. I can't remember the last time a mortal approached me. My conversations with humans have always been calculated. I always had an end goal in mind. A wrong choice for them to make.

"You seemed so fascinated," she continues. "But it is fascinating just how stupid people can be."

Despite everyone else in immodest bikinis and distasteful swimwear, she dresses for herself. She wears running shorts with an oversized t-shirt. The shirt is from a local high school and advertises their cross-country team. She brushes her long dark hair over her shoulders and sips from a glass bottle of iced coffee.

She seems so comfortable starting a conversation with me, but my heart rate quickens. Caught off guard, I search for something to say. In the meantime, her eyes lift to mine. She has eyes like the color of glass. But under her gaze, I feel like glass. My skin is a pane that allows her to stare straight into me.

"Yes. Some people are so stupid," I finally offer after a too-long pause. The sound of my voice comes across as robotic. I may be the stupid one, struck dumb by a mere human girl.

"Yeah, they are." She shakes her head, displacing small locks of ebony hair in the process. "I'll catch you around then." She turns and heads back to her friends.

By now, the humans have banded together to pull the screaming girl from the quarry. An ambulance is likely on its way, but it will take thirty minutes to reach us. She will continue to scream and cry in anguish, but I'm too distracted to enjoy it.

I am so stupid for being caught off guard. Of all the things I could have said, I eked out one stupid sentence. One small, thoughtless phrase. My gaze is involuntarily pulled to this young woman. She stands chatting with a group of other girls. My girl makes the others look vapid in comparison. Her clothing choices are more modest, only offering me glimpses of her toned thighs and thin arms. Her gestures are more refined. Each expression that crosses her face shows a full reflection of emotions.

One of the vapid girls makes a small motion towards me. My girl turns towards me and our eyes meet. Blood pulses through my limbs, but I manage to bring my hand up to wave. She repeats the gesture before turning back to her friend.

I tear my eyes from the girls to glance at the water. The blue sheet is still. No one is up for swimming after what they have seen. Well, at least while the victim's cries continue to echo over the trees. It kills everyone's good time. But once the ambulance takes her away, she will be forgotten and the cycle will repeat. Humans are so predictable.

Well, humans typically are predictable, but I didn't expect to be approached today. Oddly enough, I liked it. Listening to my girl's voice was an unexpected gift. The joy it brought parallels that of someone stumbling down the ledge.

I need to plan my next move. Should I approach her? Should I wait until after her friends leave and she is alone again? I don't even know her name. That would be a good question to start with. Do I need to prepare more questions to keep the conversation going? Should I ask about her school? The name of it was plastered on her t-shirt. That is a good place to start.

I turn back to where she was standing, but she is gone. The girls had picked up their things and left while I was in thought. Heat flashes through my chest. I was too slow and now the nameless girl is gone.

Each clear day that summer, I return to the quarry. No longer interested in the cliff, I scour the faces of each person. Her face is never among them. On days when the sky is overcast, I visit the local mall. My eyes scan the crowds, but I have no luck. I try bookstores and coffee shops. Hip restaurants and movie theaters. Everything else falls away. The search becomes my life. After many years walking this earth, I have found something more powerful to worship.

I welcome the shorter days and drier breezes because I have the name of her high school. On the first day of class, I am right in front of the school. And my patience is rewarded. My breath leaves my body upon seeing her again. Her long hair is pulled into a ponytail that bounces behind her. Tall socks are molded to her shapely calves. Below her skirt, a small glimpse of her thighs is revealed.

"Hi," I interject as she walks by me on her way in. "What's your name?"

"Josie," she replies. Her eyes move up to my face before traveling down and back up again. "You look a little old for a student."

"Just walking through the neighborhood." I put on my cheeriest face.

"Cool." She shakes her head, which gently tousles her hair. "Well, I've got to get to class."

"Bye Josie," I wave at her back.

Josie. I now have a name. And I know where to find her. Classes end at three, so after wandering for a few hours, I return to my position by the front gate. I wait patiently with visions of walking Josie home, but she isn't among the crowds drifting past me.

I walk around the school fence to a series of recreational fields. Groups of students are warming up for various sports. Boys shaped like squares toss a football. Curvy young women count aloud to coordinated movements. A dozen thin males run past, their shirts hanging from their lean frames. They are soon followed by a group of jogging girls, their long toned legs pushing them forward. And there I find Josie. The most beautiful of them all. Her hair is pulled back loosely from her face. Graceful legs fly forward from rounded hips. Heavy breathing is the only sign of exertion. I continue to watch her until they make a turn beyond my line of sight.

The next morning finds this suitor staying stoically by the school gates again. Standing straight, shoulders back, I scan the faces of the flood of students. I am a statue whose spell can only be broken by the sight of one girl. Arm in arm, Josie walks up while deep in conversation with another girl. A girl so vapid she is unmemorable.

"Josie," my voice booms through their conversation.

Josie whips her face to meet mine. Her hair flows around her shoulders like a sheer curtain in the wind. I produce a deep red rose and pass it to her. Her thin white fingers delicately take the offering from my hands.

"Will you have dinner with me this Saturday, Josie?" I plea.

"Oh, um, we're going out of town this weekend to visit my grandparents," she nods as her sentence tapers off.

"Next time then." I smile and offer a small bow.

"We have to get to class now," her little friend interrupts and pulls Josie away. I wave at Josie as she is dragged away and she raises her hand in return.

Today is Friday. It's the last day I can see Josie before we must spend two days apart. The few moments I have been able to steal are not enough. There are so many things to keep us separated. She is choosing her classes, friends, and family over me. I don't think she realizes the depth of my feelings for her. Once she does, I will be the clear choice. We can leave all this behind and devote ourselves to each other.

I must draw her in further. I need to prove to her what a wonderful companion I can be, despite my flaws. I ponder, what would wow her? More flowers? No, that doesn't seem thoughtful enough. Josie runs cross-country after school. If she saw me cheering for her, she would notice how supportive I am. She would think I am more deserving of her.

First, I must find the perfect spot to cheer for Josie. While the students are in their classes, I discreetly walk the school grounds. I head under the bleachers. Looking through the horizontal seating, I imagine Josie running by. I imagine her toned thighs flexing and releasing under her thin shorts. But these bleachers would offer too many distractions. Nearby, the cheerleaders would be shouting and the football players would be crashing. The din would cover my cheers. I walk out from under the bleachers.

Ahead, I make out a trail trampled into the grass. This trail heads into a thin patch of trees where the grass line stops and a dirt path begins. The path is short, ending at a silver metal gate where the sidewalk begins. I imagine the runners heading out this gate each afternoon.

The soft green grass before the trees offers the perfect spot to wait for Josie. After her practice one day, I could lay down a blanket. I could bring a spread of delights. There would be fresh-squeezed lemonade, sandwiches cut into triangles, and ripe fruits. We would sit side-by-side, watching the sunset. I would wrap my arm over her shoulder and use my hand to bring her face to mine. Her lips would be so soft and full as she met my kiss.

It's the perfect spot for our relationship to bloom. But for now, I will play the role of supportive suitor. I sit in the grass and wait. The ground feels soft beneath me and the trees behind me offer shade from the August sun. I allow myself to sink into the ground. Closing my eyes, I doze off.

A sharp kick to my foot wrenches me from my gentle slumber. Grimacing over me is a middle-aged wrench. Her lips are pursed as if she is sucking a lemon. Large glasses are precariously perched on her nose. Her thin body is painfully angled.

"You need to leave," she spits out.

"I'm waiting for someone," I reply gracefully.

"I don't care. Leave now or I will call the police for trespassing."

"There is no need for that," I coolly reply while keeping rage from seeping into my voice. "I am leaving now."

I stand and walk through the trees. I pass through the gate and continue walking. Her eyes glare at me until I am out of sight.

Friday evening rolls around and I am bummed. All my efforts to impress Josie have gotten me nowhere. How wonderful it will be when we finally are together. I picture her large doll-like eyes staring deeply into mine. Her rounded lips would part to expose small pearls of teeth. I would push her silken hair from her face. Tucking the stand behind her ear, I would wrap my hand around her neck in the same motion. Pulling her face to mine, we would kiss deeply.

But there seems to be some force keeping us apart. It has foiled all my attempts to show Josie how much I care for her. If the depth of my affections were known, she would throw herself from the cliffs into the waters of my love.

I try to shake the thoughts of Josie from my mind. I need a distraction. It is Friday night after all. I consider my options. There are various bars and hideaways in town, but I much rather head for something secluded. The old witch's house fits the bill.

The old witch's house sits far from town at the end of an old gravel road by a small pond. It is surrounded by the same stretch of forest that encompasses my beloved quarry. Abandoned for years, the wooden structure appears to be sinking into itself. The paint is gone and the exposed wood is rotting. Several windows are broken, but the roof still offers protection from the elements.

While the house is uninhabitable, it is perfect for teenage sins. Perfect for anything that they are itching to commit away from their parents' prying eyes. Meaning, it is their go-to for parties. drinking, drugs, and sex. Many joke that when they throw a party so great that the devil himself arrives, the house will fall and finally rest.

For me, it is the perfect place to help others make bad decisions. Handing someone a little too much to drink ensures that while they may be able to see tomorrow, the family in the minivan traveling at the same time won't. Passing a baggy of white powder to sheltered young people ensures that all their parents' dreams die. Giving out small colored pills makes individuals defend themselves from dangers that only exist in their minds. Excited by the possibilities, I pack my backpack with things that may be useful: several bottles of cheap liquor, baggies of pills and powders, and even a knife, in case I find someone that needs one.

Crossing the threshold of the ruinous home, I am recognized by many. Several greet me with a wordless smile and a pat on the back. My favorites frown when they spy my visage and subtly try to walk to other rooms. Some even walk out the back door and leave. Nothing makes me prouder than a job well done.

I walk past throngs of young adults absorbed in their conversations while passing the contents of my backpack into open hands. Red Solo cups are filled, small tablets are placed into gaping mouths, and a few joints are passed among small circles. I make my way to a gray sagging couch. Sitting on the couch I feel like a diver sinking into the water. The lip-locked couple at the other end of the couch notices the couch settling as I sit. After a glance in my direction and another between each other, the male grabs the young woman's hand and drags her away, searching for a more secluded spot.

I watch the humans throughout their party. If I sit very still, almost no one notices me. Those that do open their hands in my direction. Like Santa Claus, I reach into my bag and place a gift into their open palm.

The door opens and my heart stops before my head realizes why. Among a pack of overdressed young women stands Josie. Her hair falls into curls, framing her face like a dark hood. She is wearing lipstick in the color of dried blood. A tight black dress caresses the contours of her juvenile body. Beautiful.

I cannot stop the small smile that passes my lips. She must have lied about her grandparents to surprise me tonight. I am a regular at the witch's house, and my reputation precedes me. There must be no other explanation.

Like a predator, I deftly move past the partiers in silence. I fill the space next to Josie. I am even able to lean over her head and inhale the sweet smell of her hairspray before she notices my presence.

"Oh, it's you," she breathes out.

I pass one of the other girls a bottle from my bag. She lets out an excited squeal before leading the others deeper into the house. Angling my body and stepping forward, I lead Josie into a corner where we can talk.

"I didn't expect to see you here." I lean over her. "It was quite the surprise."

"Oh, yeah, I decided to come along at the last minute, but I can't stay long," she looks up into my face.

"Well, we must make the most of it then. What's your pleasure?" I ask while reaching into my bag.

"Something to drink, I guess," she replies with an uncertainty that is born in innocence.

"Try this." I pass her a large glass bottle filled with clear liquid.

Josie opens it and takes a sip. Her face scrunches with disgust.

"Not a fan of vodka?" I probe, while lightly laughing at her expense.

Gently taking the bottle from her soft hands, I lift it to my lips. One gulp, then two, then three splashes down my throat.

"That is how it's done." I pass the bottle back to Josie. "Try again."

Obediently, she takes another sip. Frowning, she shakes her head.

"It's still not good," she replies, handing the bottle back.

"Ah, well it was worth a try. What's next?" I offer.

"I should try to find my friends." Josie tries to look over my shoulder.

"Don't worry about them. They're having fun. Besides, you never spend any time with me." I try to put on my best pout. Josie lets out a small giggle.

"How about a walk? It's beautiful out tonight!"

Josie shyly nods. I wrap my hand around hers and pull her towards the door.

Darkness blankets the woods outside the house. It fills the spaces between the cars and lays across the ground. The house sits like a beacon in a world of black. I pull Josie towards a small path descending into the woods. My eyes adjust well to the faint light from the moon, but for Josie's sake, I pull out my phone. The flashlight in my phone is bright, but it only illuminates a small area. I point it at the ground, and it lights our path.

Excitement presses against my chest. Finally, I am alone with the object of my desires. As I guide her further into the woods, I lead her in conversation. Women love talking about themselves, so it is my duty to ask questions. I ask about her school and her classes. I ask about her hobbies and cross country. I ask about friends and family, all the while learning more about this beautiful lady.

Josie's replies are like how a new driver commands a vehicle. When her answers flow too quickly, she stops then slowly accelerates back to speed. As we walk, her hand feels so small in mine, but she doesn't offer any resistance to my hand pulling her forward.

Ahead, the trees give way. The ground drops down into the pit of the quarry. Filled with water, the quarry reflects the moon and stars. An otherworldly glow lays against the night. It's magical. It's romantic.

I turn off the light. Josie interrupts her latest reply as she feels the energy of the space. But the night is not quiet. Crickets, frogs, cicadas, and other creatures act as our orchestra. They come together to compose the symphony of a late summer night.

"This is where we first met." I wrap my arms around Josie.

She pulls back, looking squarely into my face. "I guess it is."

Exhaling, I close my eyes and lean towards Josie. Admittedly, I am proud to have found such a romantic spot for our first kiss. But to my surprise, our lips don't make contact. Josie pulls away further until she breaks free from my arms.

Josie looks so small and so guilty. "I'm sorry if I led you on, but I'm just not into you that way."

Anger boils at the edges of my vision. My body and head fill with warmth. "What do you mean by that?!" I exclaim.

"I'm sorry, but I'm not interested in older men." She looks down at the ground, not at my face.

Stupid. Stupid. Stupid. I am so stupid. I let myself develop feelings for such an insipid creature. A creature so below me. I am ashamed. How could she deny me like this? She is too stupid to see what she is missing. She is too cruel to see the pain she is causing me.

Without thought, as if on their own will, my hands wrap around her neck. Feebly, she tries to smack my hands away. She tries to claw her fingers under mine. It is a weak attempt, as weak as she is worthless. Squeezing my fingers deeper into her throat, her gasps sound more desperate. Her hands flail faster. Smacking my arms and my chest, her attacks grow slower before fully stopping. Her body grows weak. She falls into me. Her legs are no longer able to support her.

Placing her on the ground, I grab my backpack. I move my hands along the ground until I find a large rock. I add the rock to my backpack and I repeat the process until I have a few good-sized stones in the bag.

Now I turn to the body. She is very light, so I easily drag her by the shoulders into the shallow quarry water. I thread each arm through the backpack straps. Then I push her off past the drop-off where the water goes down for dozens of feet. A few bubbles float up to the surface as the body sinks to the bottom of the quarry.

The deed is done. My anger has dissipated. A slight disappointment replaces it. I liked this quarry. I liked this town. But several people saw me leave with Josie so it's time to move on. Time for bigger things. Perhaps it has been time all along. I have grown too comfortable here. Besides, this isn't the only town with a quarry.

Stronger by the Day

Friday night after work finds me sitting at my favorite spot at my favorite bar. I like this spot for several reasons. I can strike up a conversation with Jay behind the counter, and I can watch whatever sport was playing on the TV behind him. Tonight, it is college football.

Just past seven thirty, a gorgeous woman strolls up to the bar and sits on the stool next to mine. She has everything a man needs. Thick black hair frames her face in strong waves. Large, dark eyes stare out at the world. Soft, plump lips frown. Her outfit reveals a modest amount of cleavage, and her toned arms and legs are on full display. But whatever beauty she has is marred with her expression of disgust. Disgust pointed towards me. As a man in my fifties with a beer belly, I am aware that I am no looker, but I am still taken aback by her rudeness. She chose the seat next to me when there are many others available. It puts a sour taste in my mouth.

"Do you know who I am?" she asks me.

I think about it. I don't think I've ever seen this woman before in my life. I would have remembered her if I had.

"I don't believe so," I reply.

Her look of disgust turns to outright malice.

"I am your worst nightmare."

"Is this a joke? Who set you up to this?" I try to chuckle away the eerie feeling she gives me.

"It's not a joke," she flatly replies. "You are a worthless cockroach. Your stupidity and carelessness destroyed something far better than yourself. You took everything from me. For that, I will take everything from you. I suggest you show remorse and kill yourself now because I will kill you as soon as I get the chance. Your time is ticking down. I am getting stronger by the day!" she spits before storming out.

"What the fuck was that?" I ask Jay.

"Bitches are crazy." He shakes his head and pours me another drink.

I put back a few more beers before stumbling out of the bar.

"Be careful out there," Jay shouts at me on my way out. "A couple got hit by a drunk driver last night."

I wave him off. If I couldn't drive, I would know it. As the door closes behind me, I feel a drastic change in the atmosphere. The bar behind me was bathed in a warm yellow glow. With comfortable seats and jovial conversations, it almost felt like being gathered in the living room after a family meal. On the other hand, the parking lot lacks any semblance of comfort. The cold wind nips at my face and the silence feels harsh. A few white lights illuminate empty parking spaces. I am alone except for a single figure sitting on a bus bench. I think of the woman from earlier and a shiver shakes my body. I hurry to my car and lock the door.

Driving home absorbs my attention. Navigating the dark and winding roads takes care at any time. Navigating these roads after a few drinks takes focus. There is one curve that gives me pause. The side of the road drops steeply into a small lake. But the concentration puts my mind at ease. When I make it home, I am able to fall asleep moments after crawling into bed.

"You are worthless scum," I hear someone shout into my dreams.

My body jumps up and I fumble for my lamp. A soft light fills my room. It is empty. My panting breaths are the only sound filling the space. The sheets are sticking to my sweaty skin. A dull ache fills my chest. It is times like these when I wish there was a wife lying next to me. Her eyes would fill with concern and she would rub my back. Assure me that it was just a bad dream. But I am alone in this bed.

I should be laughing at myself. That crazy bitch has gotten to me. I rack my brain. What could I have done to her? Maybe she had me mistaken for someone else. I leave the lamp on and settle back into my sheets. I stare at the ceiling and let it fill my vision. Letting my thoughts become absorbed into the ceiling, I fall back asleep.

Coming into consciousness the next morning, the first thing I am aware of is the ache in my head. It is dull, but it is everywhere. The sunlight streams into my room, shimmering with floating dust. I need water, coffee, and to piss.

It is Saturday, which means I have work around the house to do. I make a mental list: laundry, mowing the lawn, wash the car, clean the floors, and wash the dishes. I start by throwing my clothes into the washing machine with some detergent. Next, I move to start unloading the dishes.

Looking up, I see her through my kitchen window. The same dark hair frames her furrowed brows and dark eyes brimming with hatred. Her right arm is extended and a noose swings from her hand.

This is ridiculous. Grabbing my gun, I check to make sure it is loaded before charging outside. I run to where she had been moments ago, but she is gone.

"I've got a gun," I shout. "You better leave me alone."

I briefly consider searching for her, but she is very fast and quiet. The last thing I want is for this crazy bitch to get the better of me. Heading back inside, I pull the deadbolt to seal her out. I run to each window to get a look at every angle of my property. Two empty cars are parked along the street. My neighbors' yards are vacant. A small collection of trees stands alone. I can't find her, but I don't let my guard down.

I move from window to window. It feels like hours are passing. I keep my gun at my side, partially hoping I find her and partially hoping I don't. After a few cycles, I come to the realization that she has trapped me in my own home. She has me acting like a mouse, afraid of the cat. But I am not to be hunted. I am not prey. She is the one who should be afraid of me. Why should I be afraid of a small girl with a noose?

I almost laugh at myself for being so stupid. The tension in my shoulders releases. I crack open a beer and sit on my couch, deciding to relax. Flipping through the channels on my TV, I pass the news, pass some dumb kids' cartoon, and finally settle on a sitcom rerun. Screw the chores. There is always tomorrow. Who could be productive when there is a psycho like her on the loose? I open another beer and let episode after episode play.

The pitter patter of footsteps draws me from my stupor. Grabbing my gun, I am instantly awake. I slowly prowl the rooms of my home with my finger sitting lightly on the trigger. My living room and kitchen are empty. Pulling open the pantry door, I am greeted with nothing but canned and boxed food. My garage door is still deadbolted. Behind my shower curtain and inside my bathroom are vacant.

Flipping the lights in my bedroom illuminates the noose hanging from the ceiling fan. This is the final straw. I flip up the bed and tear the clothes from my closet. But there is nothing. She isn't here.

Fifteen minutes after calling, an officer pulls into my driveway. I tell him about the girl from the bar and the noose. He takes notes in a small notebook that he pulled from his front pocket. Occasionally nodding and asking follow-up questions, he fills several pages. He offers to walk around my yard and house. We can't find a trace of the girl except for the noose in my bedroom. The officer asks to see the garage, so I unlock the door and wave him in.

"You've been in an accident recently?" he asks.

"No," I reply, "why do you ask?"

He gestures to the side of my car. My blood runs cold in shock, but it quickly heats in rage.

"That bitch tore up the side of my car," the words are a force tearing through my mouth.

The entire side of my car is scratched and dented. It is almost as if it is caving in on itself. How did I not hear her doing this?

"I don't think a girl did this to your car. She would have to be pretty strong for that. Look, there are several transfers of red paint." The officer points to several scratches.

"Well, I didn't do this myself," I shout. "She must have taken a red bat, tire iron, or something to my car."

The officer takes a deep breath, "We don't know how this woman got into your home and we don't know where she currently is. Why don't you come with me back to the station?"

I nod. I hate to sound like a sissy, but that girl is angry and evidently quite strong. A woman that had the strength to beat up my car like that should not be taken lightly. If she snuck into my room at night with a knife, I might be done for. Leaving with the officer seems like the safest option.

The officer keeps his hands rigidly on the wheel, but his eyes continually shift from the road to me.

"Where were you two nights ago?" he asks, breaking the silence of our drive.

"Two nights ago?" I shake off the question. "This woman just entered my life last night. I'm sure of it. I've already tried to rack my brain to figure out what I did to upset her so much, but I can't think of anything to explain that crazy woman." Desperation sits at the edges of my voice.

"Why don't we start with two nights ago?" His lack of emotion is a stark contrast to mine.

"It was a normal day. I went to work. I grabbed dinner followed by a few drinks at the bar and then I went home."

The police cruiser sways with the winding road. Car and road dance intimately, but one wrong move would send us down the incline into the lake.

"You didn't see anything suspicious? What about on your drive home?"

"Nothing comes to mind, officer."

He sighs. "A young couple was driving home along this road two nights ago. We don't know how, but their car ended up in the lake." His eyes meet mine for a brief moment before returning to the road. "Their car was bright red. Would have been hard to miss."

I shake my head. "I didn't see it."

"The young man died immediately, but the girl is in a coma." He turns in my direction. I look into his eyes and can see where this is going.

"What are you accusing me of?" I shout.

"It seems like you might have a guilty conscience." His statement strikes me like an ax.

"What kind of shoddy police work is this?" Rage fills my body and throws force behind my words. "This crazy bitch has been threatening me and you think she's just a figment of my imagination? I bet you she hit them and is trying to frame me for the crime. She beat up my car to make it look like it was in an accident! Don't you see that she is trying to ruin my life? And you think she isn't real? Pull over, I'm getting out."

I slam the door behind me and head towards town on foot. I want to punch that self-righteous little officer's face. I want to strangle that crazy bitch's throat. Shaking with rage, I need to break something.

I take a deep breath instead. I need a plan. I need to prove that the bitch is real and she is out to get me. If she pushed that car off the road, she must have had a reason. Maybe she keeps a list of people who wronged her. She checks their names off as she hurts them, torments them, and destroys them. She thought she could kill two birds with one stone by framing me for the accident, but she is wrong. I'll start at the hospital. The comatose girl must be the missing link. I need to find out who would want to hurt her.

With a purpose, the walk to town becomes much easier. In town, I buy a newspaper. I flip through it looking for mentions of the accident. I find a single article. The article doesn't supply much more information than the officer. It does include a picture of a red partially submerged car as well as the name of the young woman: Mia Stratton.

Slipping into the hospital is surprisingly easy. I just tell the front desk that I am Mia's uncle.

"We've been expecting you," the young woman behind the desk replies cheerfully.

A nurse leads me to Mia's room, but as we get closer, something begins to feel off. It almost seems a bit too quiet. The weight of the air seems to press against my chest. I shake the feeling off. Of course it's quiet, we are going to see a coma patient.

Ice races down my spine as we enter her room. An invisible hand grips my heart. There she is. My tormenter sleeps before me. Her eyes are closed and her pouty lips are set in a deep frown, but her dark curls frame her face. A sleeping beauty.

"Are you sure this is the right room?" I ask the nurse.

Confusion furrows her brow. She looks down at my tormenter before replying, "Yes, this is the woman from the car accident."

34

The nurse turns from Mia to look at me. "Is your drinking causing memory problems?"

I freeze in surprise. Are the nurses in on it too?

"I remember seeing you a few months ago. You were so drunk when they brought you in that you didn't know who you were."

"I don't know what you're talking about," I sputter, "but I would like to be alone with my niece."

The nurse shakes her head. "It must have been someone else. I'll be down the hall if you need me."

She departs, leaving me alone with the sleeping woman. My heart beats in my ears. Tremors vibrate in my hands. But it isn't hot rage I feel, it's fear. Did the nurse really remember me from months ago? It was a one-time thing. I typically hold my alcohol better, but I blacked out. I can't tell you how much I drank. I was fine in the morning. They could have dropped me off at home instead of the hospital, really.

I thought back to Thursday night. I don't remember how I got home that night either. I remember drinking at the bar and I remember waking up Friday morning in my bed. My memory is filled with black holes.

Suddenly, the walls of the room come crashing in on me as my lungs are trying to escape my chest. No matter how hard I inhale, my lungs are empty. I am drowning without any water. How did I get home Thursday night? I beg my brain to return an answer. Instead, something is squeezing my heart. Is it panic?

I look down at Mia. Sleeping beauty's lips turn up in a smile. My chest hurts. Fire fills my lungs. The nurse bursts into the room. She calls for help. Darkness replaces the world around me, but not before I see sleeping beauty's eyes flutter open.

Stroll

Is there a more satisfying sound than footsteps against a hard surface? Each step echoes and fills the space around it. Each loud footfall confers confidence. The idea that I belong there and I know it. I have nothing to hide. This contrasts with footsteps against a soft surface. The small pads against dirt, the slight crisps against snow, or the gentle crunch of leaves confers subterfuge. The idea that I am trespassing in a space. I know I don't belong here and I am trying to minimize my presence. I will face into my surroundings and disappear.

I love the path beside the river because it is paved with hard stones, allowing each step to announce one's presence. It must have taken years to complete, but I believe the labor was worthwhile to hear each satisfying step.

Each evening, after the warm orbs of lamps dot the streets, I walk. I walk along the river and I let my thoughts drift. Looking beyond the path, the river's water flows black as asphalt. The occasional splash reminds me of the river's natural origin. I'm seldom alone along this path, but people are sparse. A giggling couple with linked arms may find a private bench. Those who can't sleep are often meandering along. Exhausted service staff silently head home. Very few have offered conversation as I've walked. Everyone seems wrapped up in their own heads. This night is different. This night I hear subtle footsteps behind me. I turn to face their owner.

"Lovely evening we're having here," a stocky form throws the words across the darkness.

"Indeed," I reply, not taking my eyes from his frame.

"My dog shook off his lead a few moments ago. Have you seen any dogs pass this way?"

"I have not."

"Are you in a rush? Would you mind helping me look for him?" the figure asks.

"Sure, I can help."

"I'd appreciate it. Let's look closer to the river." The man steps next to me and places his hand on my back. With gentle pressure, he pushes me forward.

"Do you often walk alone at night?" he quizzes. As we approach a lamp, his features begin to reveal themselves. He is stocky, with dark hair and a square chin.

"Every night. I enjoy the peace."

"But surely you have a husband waiting for you at home." He looks down at me.

"Not even a dog waits for me. I prefer the solitude."

"That seems a bit dangerous. You know there is a serial killer on the loose." He shakes his head.

"I think more than two murders are necessary for someone to be classified as a serial killer."

He stops for a moment. "Death is death, regardless of how many people have gone before you."

"I refuse to live my life in fear." I step to the side, letting his hand fall.

"So, you're not afraid of anything then?" he asks.

I shake my head. "I've done what is necessary to assure my survival."

He pauses. His silence falls heavy on my shoulders. The river gurgles. Standing still, the world shifts between fading from consciousness and focusing. Golden pyramids beneath each lamp dot the path, and yet it isn't enough. Darkness patiently sits outside the circle of light.

"It's so quiet here," he interrupts the void with his spoken thought.

"I can't hear anything, human or dog. Perhaps you should try somewhere else."

"But I'm enjoying our conversation so much." He gestures towards me.

"But it won't help you find your dog," I scold.

Shaking his head, he looks around us. "Don't be so serious."

I swallow. There is no dog. And there doesn't appear to be anyone else on this path either. I am alone with this man. I catch him staring at my face, which betrays my train of thought. A small smile slices his face in two. Placing his hand on the small of my back again, he pushes me forward.

"You've thought a lot about fear." He eases us back into a stroll. Two sets of muted footsteps patter softly.

"I've thought about how to best live my life, fully and with purpose." I keep my voice steady.

"Walking alone through secluded areas in the dark is an odd way to live purposely and fully." His voice is flat.

"This walk is very important, though."

"How so?" He smiles, bemused.

I turn to look him fully in the face. "I'm somewhat of a Utilitarian."

"A what? I've never heard of that. Is that some sort of religion?"

"Utilitarian. It's more of an ethical framework than a religion. There is no God to worship and nothing after death. With religion, there often are too many churches filled with hypocrites. They believe that since they are saved or chosen by God, they are good. They will do horrible things: lie, cheat, steal, tear others down, and even kill. All while looking at themselves in the mirror believing that they are a good person. When you believe that you are good, you don't try to be good. Religion stagnates people morally."

He nods. "And your framework solves this?"

We walk onto a small bridge. Black water churns below us. I stop and lay my arms on the rail.

"Utilitarianism," I begin, "defines our purpose in life to be increasing the good in the world and decreasing the bad. It is an active, continual process that only ends upon our deaths. We must think consciously about our actions, weighing potential benefits against potential consequences. Selfish choices must be limited."

"But why? Why not be selfish? Why not do what's best for you?"

"Humans are innately social beings. We don't often try to make it on our own. We quickly recognized the utility of societies. Society provides protection and shares labor. And often what benefits society will benefit you, too."

"But there will always be people that will take advantage of others in their society."

"You are right, but there will also always be people willing to help."

He scoffs. "So, you would just let the users run amok? Taking, hunting, and killing as they please?"

It is my turn to smile. "You misunderstand me. I weigh the benefits and consequences of my actions. Sometimes doing something bad will cause a lot of good for others."

"I don't understand."

I turn towards the stranger. Fading scratches cross his hands and face. Staring into his eyes, I lean closer to him. "You will."

His eyes widen and a gasp falls from his lips. Like a fish out of water, he struggles for breath. He struggles to speak. I pull my knife from his stomach before plunging it into his chest. Blood rushes from his torso and onto my hands, making them sticky. I plant my feet firmly onto the bridge's stone surface and push him towards the railing. Caught by surprise, he doesn't struggle. He stumbles backward. Before he regains balance, I lift his legs and tip him over the rail. The resulting splash is so loud that I look around to see if anyone heard. But just as before, I am alone. Alone as I continue my walk into the night.

The Case

My wife was convinced we needed a romantic getaway. As if a trip was enough to save my marriage. I was skeptical. Aren't we the same people on a beach as we are at home? Our problems don't go away because we are hundreds of miles away. But I was willing to give it a try and agreed to go. She planned the trip for the two of us. I have to admit that it will be nice to be the center of her attention for the first time in years. Since the birth of our daughter, I've been demoted to second place in her heart.

To be honest, I wanted a son, but my wife is satisfied with one child. Her daughter is her world and nothing can stand between that. Clara is only seven, but my wife has molded the child into her image. Her daughter is a miniature of herself. Quiet, self-sufficient, and neat, Clara doesn't seem like a child. Clara would sooner have a conversation with adults than play with other children.

I find it hard to relate to Clara. She is so attached to her mother that there seems to be no room for me. It's almost as if I am living as my wife's sperm donor. But a trip could change things. We could reignite a spark between us. I could convince my wife to try for another child. A boy that would take after me. A son, who would want to spend time playing catch or watching the game. Leave the girls to themselves because we wouldn't need them.

Ultimately, the trip does change things, but not how I expected. We arrive at the small south-of-the-border resort town late at night. It is too dark to see anything. Under shadow are white-plastered shops with light blue roofs. Hidden by the night are cobbled pathways, inviting a stroll through the town. Even the ocean offers a blank horizon. Too late for dinner, we collapse into bed.

Morning brings bright sunlight into the room. Despite the late arrival, my wife awakes full of energy. She is eager to visit the white sand beaches, but I want to rest a bit longer. She is convinced we need to leave early to get a good spot, whatever that means. The ocean goes on for miles. There are miles of good spots. I am unable to convince her, so I tell her to go on without me and I will meet her there later. She leaves reluctantly.

Once I feel fully awake, I dress for the beach and head out. In the sunlight, I am able to appreciate the quaint town. Strolling slowly, I am met with the sounds of sea breezes and the smell of salt. Buildings are built haphazardly, yet flow with the scenery. It is as if they emerged from the sand fully formed. The white, blue, and beige color pallet of the town matches the shore.

I am alone for most of my stroll, following the meandering pathways. I find a small bench and sit down. Silently, I merge into the scenery behind me. I watch gulls pick at the ground and fly away. But, for the most part, I sit alone with my thoughts. It is peaceful.

My peace is interrupted by a beaten and bloodied man running through the street. Continually turning to look over his shoulder, he never notices me. I don't move as he passes by. Without a sound, I watch as he places a briefcase between a planter and a wall before running past.

Moments later, footsteps clatter and echo through the street. Two running men come into view. They slow as they approach me. To them, I am not invisible. They say something in Spanish, but I shake my head, unable to understand. I point in the direction of the first man and they run off to continue the chase.

I wait to leave my bench until I can no longer hear or see the men. With care, I grab the case from its hiding place and make my way back to our hotel room, careful to avoid all people. In the safety of my room, I shut the drapes and lock the door. Placing the case on the bed, I open it and am met with awe. Even stacks of money fill the case. I count it all. One million American dollars. A windfall.

I text my wife that we need to leave now. I run through the room packing our things. By the time she returns everything is in our suitcases. Anything she wants to say about leaving early falls from her face when she sees my expression. I am filled with excitement and anxiety that borders on mania. We sit silently in our car for several hours as I drive. I don't want to mention the briefcase to my wife until we make it home. Upon hearing the news, my wife doesn't share my enthusiasm.

"Shouldn't you give it to the authorities?" she asks.

She is skeptical, but I go on about all the ways the money could improve things. We could buy a bigger house or nicer cars. Our daughter could go to the best private schools and attend college debt-free. My wife finally stops arguing against keeping the money. But she cautions against using the money immediately.

"It would look suspicious," she advises "Let's hide it and hold onto it for a while."

So I hide it. I place the case deep into the back of our closet under boxes of junk. There it sits, untouched for weeks, until the text messages arrive.

WE KNOW YOU TOOK OUR CASE. MAKE ARRANGEMENTS TO RE-TURN THE CASE IMMEDIATELY AND UNTOUCHED AND NOTHING WILL HAPPEN TO YOU.

I never reply. I merely confirm the case is safe. They must have gotten my number from the hotel, but I don't think they can reach me now that I am out of the country. I think little of the message until the next one arrives days later.

WE HAVE YOUR DAUGHTER.

I thought it was another scare tactic until my wife calls in hysterics. Our daughter wasn't at the school pickup line. No teacher, staff member, or child knew where she had gone. One moment Clara was waiting with the other children, the next moment she wasn't.

I confess to my wife about the messages. Her anger flows forth like a fountain. Crazed like a maenad, I think she is going to rip my head off. Instead, she takes my phone and negotiates my daughter's return. My daughter's captors name the place and time. They also emphasize that we can't involve the police and should only bring the case.

The time is before sunset and the place is a secluded canyon. Our car meanders up the dirt path, kicking up a trail of dust behind us. The road rises through the lonely desert as the sun sinks into the horizon. Near the top of the canyon, we pass two SUVs. Men loiter nearby and leer at our passing vehicle. Each man has a gun hanging from his torso and holstered on his side, readily available. The road curves around a bend and continues up until the men can no longer be seen behind us. At the top, the road ends where the canyon drops off. Another SUV is parked and waiting. Tinted windows hide its occupants from view. We park and exit our vehicle. I hold the case.

A man emerges from the driver's seat of the SUV. He opens the back door and roughly pulls Clara out, dragging her by the arm. She cries in pain. He walks her over to the cliff's edge.

"No guns and no police, like we agreed?" he asks.

My wife nods. "Yes, we only brought the case. Please return my daughter."

"Put the case on my car," he commands.

I comply with his order and step back towards my wife.

"Good, it was smart of you to bring our money back, but it was stupid of you to have taken it. You fucked with us and no one fucks with us for free." He spits the words out before he flings Clara over the cliff.

Time slows after Clara goes over the cliff. I never hear a cry from my wife. I never hear anything. After Clara disappears down the cliffside, my wife pushes off the ground and into the man. Off-balance, the man falls into the empty space behind him. My wife never touches the ground again as she and the man sail over the cliff's edge together. Together, they follow Clara.

I wait for another thug to emerge from the car or from up the road, but none come. Everything is still. I am the only one standing on top of the canyon now. I creep towards the edge. Despite the growing darkness, I can make out three bodies at the bottom. The man, mother, and child lie bloodied and contorted.

Looking back into the SUV, I confirm that no one is waiting there. I note that the keys sit in the cupholder. Walking around the front of the car, I observe that the glass is tinted too dark to see the driver. It is luck so good that I catch myself smiling. I place the case in the passenger seat. It should be easy enough to lose the other two SUVs on the way back. The night is ascending in the desert and they only have four headlights to see by. Driving down the canyon with my money by my side, I am off to start a brand new life.

Over the Mountain

The death of my wife is the final straw. I watched my country decay around me and I let it happen. Instead of trying to fix my circumstances, I adjusted to them. As food became scarce, I encouraged my family to wake up earlier. If they left before sunrise, they could scour whatever meager plants grew overnight. I sent them farther into the mountains in search of food. Each meal was smaller and included a weak broth to make each morsel last a little bit longer. We persevered.

And when gangs formed around us, I encouraged my family to only go out in large groups. I urged them to be cautious. I urged them to hide or submit if necessary. We survived so long like this, even as my neighbors were losing children, mothers, and fathers. But our security did not last forever.

My wife had taken our two children into the mountains to forage for edible leaves, nuts, and berries. Hours later, my son and daughter ran through our village begging for help. A man with a knife had attacked them. Their mother had urged them to run as she swung at the man.

When we found her, my wife's body was cold. The fabric of her dress clung to her, sticky with blood. Dark blood soaked the soil around her. She had been dead for hours.

It is a wake-up call. I need to take my two children and leave my home country. I've heard of families leaving before. They would hire a guide to lead them through the mountains in the north and across the border. It is a dangerous journey, but our northern neighbor is a prosperous country. In that country, there is enough to eat. There are no gangs because violent individuals meet swift ends.

I'd rather risk death for a new life than await our deaths here. It takes weeks to find a guide and I must sell most of our possessions to pay their fee and buy supplies for the trip. We need food, water, and warm, thick clothes. Snow sits on the top of the mountain year-round. After the mountain crossing, many people abandon their extra clothing and supplies. As the guides return, they gather as much as they can carry back to sell at a discount.

The frigid mountain crossing isn't the most dangerous obstacle of the trip. Past the base of the mountain range is a wide plain. The ground is flat along this plain and provides a view for many miles. The plain ends in the river that acts as the country border. Our northern neighbor discourages immigrants. The plain between the mountain and the river is heavily guarded by the dead. Instead of wasting resources on prisons, our neighbor uses their criminals. They inject their criminals with a concoction of chemicals. This injection keeps the body moving while killing the criminal's remaining humanity. Their violent urges are amplified. They kill and tear apart any living thing that crosses their path. They ignore the others of their kind, only taking heed of where the others are heading. Should they bite a survivor, they can pass on their condition. But our northern neighbor is clever. Their concoction makes the dead afraid of water. This means the dead won't cross the river behind them or over the snowy mountains in front of them. Our guide assures us that these creatures should not deter us, because once we are at the river, we are safe.

The trip will only take five days. Five days until we can begin a new life together. I am glad that my children aren't small. Trying to manage two little children on such a dangerous trip would be nearly impossible. My son is 15. His body may be lean, but his face has already matured into manhood. He projects strength and is fiercely protective of his sister. At 13, she is on the cusp of womanhood, but a lack of food stunted her growth, so she still appears childlike. She uses that to her advantage, as she continues to engage in childish games. Each morning, she runs back and forth from one end of the village to the other. She lets the other children chase her, but not even the boys can catch her. Her long legs pull her forward with each step. She isn't like a bird in flight, but rather like a rubber band snapping forward. The only signs of exertion are the breaths filling her chest like a drowning person gasping for air.

The three of us will manage. We meet our guide early in the morning. Seven others join us. Two are brothers. The next consists of a young man and his mother. The final group includes a father, his adult son, and his son's pregnant wife. Our first two days are uneventful. We walk most of the day, breaking every few hours to rest and eat. During this time, we climb over the smaller mountains near our village.

On the third day, we reach the larger mountain range. The trip becomes much harder. As we climb, our route becomes steeper. I have to use my hands to pull myself up at several points. The air is colder. Each breath of chilled air includes several knives to slice at my throat. My lips crack and bleed. But my children carry forward, and so do I.

On the fourth day, we see the watchers of the mountain. We cross over the peak and begin our descent. On our way down, dozens of human forms appear, sitting on the mountainside. Unmoving, they look like statues made of ice instead of marble. Their skin appears a pockmarked blue and gray instead of smooth ivory. Each stare down towards the plain even though the mist obscures their view. As we approach, our guide tells us not to disturb them, otherwise evil will befall us. Plagued with enough bad luck, we push our curiosity aside to keep moving forward.

The morning of the fifth day finds us at the base of the mountain and the start of the plain. Our guide tells us to leave our supplies behind, only keeping what is lightweight. He points towards the plain and tells us to keep heading in that direction. He will not travel any further with us. He tells us that if the dead see us, to run as fast as we can towards the river. Then he ascends back up the mountain, burdened with our excess supplies.

The plain is only a few miles across, but we inch forward. Our heads pivot from side to side, front to back, looking for the dead. Hours pass in silence. Then the pregnant woman stops moving.

"I see one," she whispers.

She drops to the ground, trying to blend into the landscape. But it is too late. He sees us and begins sprinting in our direction. The dead man runs far faster than the lifeless should be able to run. My heart drops in my chest. We need to get to the river.

"Run!" I push my children forward.

We run. The group moves across the plain like a wave. All I can think of is pushing forward. The river isn't in view and my lungs already ache. I can hear the dead man behind me now. He snarls and growls like a beast, frothing at the mouth. A scream interrupts from my right. I turn my head to watch the pregnant woman fall to the ground under the weight of the dead man. Her husband stops to push the dead man off, but another creature grabs him and pulls him down as well.

Still running, I look around, and to my dismay, I see many more dead heading towards us. But the path ahead of us remains clear. My children are in front of me. Nothing else matters except the three of us reaching the river. The scene behind me fades. I can barely hear the screams and snarls over my own breathing. My daughter is outpacing the rest of us. She is five feet ahead, then ten, and finally twenty. She never looks back. Her complete attention is focused forward.

The river comes into view and relief washes over me. My lungs are on fire. Each breath is agony. A little further and I can rest. But my hope transcends into horror. A beast comes from the side and tackles my son to the ground. I cover the distance between us in a matter of seconds that spans hours. Using my momentum, I run into the beast, knocking him off my son. In a blind rage, I beat the monster until it is still. I turn back to my son. He lies on the ground as still as the beast, his throat bloodied strips of skin. Glassy eyes stare back at me vacantly. My son is dead.

I stand and look at the carnage around me. Twisted and torn forms lie upon the ground. The monsters have stopped their onslaught and stand swaying gently. Blood runs from their mouths and drenches their fingers. They look like scarecrows, standing in a field of destruction. Among their vacant faces, I can't see anyone from our group. I run from body to body, confirming the dead. The beasts leave me to my work. There are eight bodies, including my son. My daughter is not among them.

I think it strange that the dead didn't attack me, but a glance at my arm reveals the awful truth. A bite mark is embedded into my flesh. I am one of them now.

I walk towards the river, but don't enter the water. I walk along the sides until I can see my daughter. She stands on the other side. I crouch low to the ground before she can see me. I observe her nervously watching the plain, trying to see those that were supposed to be behind her. Tears stain her face, but she does not dare enter the river again.

Looking back at the monsters, I decide that I can't let myself become like them. My thoughts bring me back to the statues on the mountain. I realize then what they are. A frozen warning to the next group about the dangers in front of them. With a flush of anger, I remember the guide waving us forward, leaving the warning unheeded. The same guide that refused to cross the plain with us. I decide to add my face to the warning, letting our guide know that he led another group to their deaths.

I plow my way back to the mountain, determined to make it before my transformation is complete. As I ascend the mountain, my limbs begin to stiffen in the cold. Each step becomes more difficult. The frozen wind dries my skin. Pain sears through my body. But I am determined. The day is clear and I reach the statues before nightfall. I sit on the mountain beside them.

The pain begins to numb as my limbs lock into place, but I no longer need to move. The sky is clear, affording me a wide view of the plain and beyond. The sun sets across the horizon, casting its light upon the river shimmering in pink and gold. Night falls and I make out a small fire miles beyond the river. Tears stream down my face as I think about my daughter, safely on the other side, off to start a brand new life.

Drenched

If you're not careful and you noclip out of reality in the wrong areas, you'll end up in the Backrooms, where it's nothing but the stink of old moist carpet, the madness of mono-yellow, the endless background noise of fluorescent lights at the maximum hum-buzz, and approximately six hundred million square miles of randomly segmented empty rooms to be trapped in.

God save you if you hear something wandering around nearby because it sure as hell heard you.

— Anonymous 4chan user, May 14, 2019

Chapter 1

I stop to examine the sign.

$$2731 - 2749$$
$$<———————$$
$$2751 - 2779$$
$$———————>$$

I can't prevent the frustrated sigh that passes my lips. I am already running late and this sign doesn't help. The location of room 2713 remains a mystery. Rather than turning left or right, I turn around and walk back the way I came.

I walk past rooms numbered 2728, 2725, and 2719. Following the hallway left and right and left again, I watch the decreasing numbers. Pulling my phone from my bag, I check the time. The interview starts at 11:00 and it is already 10:57.

I have to pick up the pace. I am already walking as fast as I can without running. My body jerks up and down. The thin yellowing carpet muffles my steps as I stride past the elevator that I rode up. Passing room 2750, I almost stop in confusion. Am I lost or are the rooms out of order? But I glance around and see 2716. Pivoting, I walk towards 2716, then 2715, and 2714, before finally finding 2713.

I pull out my phone. 11:00. Perfect. I knock three times.

"Come in," returns a hoarse voice.

I step into room 2713.

"Jordan, right? You're late," the man behind the desk says. "If you're not early, you're late." He gestures to a seat.

His fingers are swollen and pink, like little sausages ready to burst. These pink sausages are attached to a pink arm. His pink arms emerge from a wrinkled yellow short-sleeve button-down. Also emerging from the sallow shirt is a round head. He has thick jowls permanently set in a scowl, a short round nose, small beady eyes, and a greasy comb-over.

To complement the pink and yellow hues of the man, his office color pallet consists of yellow and brown. Yellowed carpet meets yellowing walls under yellow fluorescent lights. The dark brown desk is chipped at the corners, revealing light brown particle board. Papers are scattered across the desk. Imprints of past coffee cups are distributed across both the desk and the papers. My immediate reaction is disgust, but I have to swallow my first impression and sit down.

"When your shift starts at 10 PM, you need to be at your seat, headset on, computer up," the man explains. "None of this showing up at 10 PM and taking your time getting set up. Understood?"

I nod.

"Good. I'm the manager here. You can call me Mr. Richards. The night shift runs from 10 PM until 6:30 the following morning. You have thirty minutes for a meal. You clock in and out, so I will know if you are late. Do you understand?"

"I understand."

"Good, good. Now, this is the third shift, and we don't appreciate any sleeping on the job. The first time we catch it, your pay is docked for that night. The second time and you're out. This isn't a three-strike system."

I nod again and try to strain a smile.

"Alright. Now, this job is so simple you don't need a brain to do it. You got a brain, darling?"

I can't stop my face from blushing and my nostrils from flaring. I have to swallow again before the rest of my emotions show on my face.

"Yes sir, I have a brain," I reply flatly. I wish I didn't need this job.

"I thought so. Now, when someone calls, it will pop up on the computer screen. If they are calling from the phone number in their file, their information will pop up on the screen. If their information doesn't pop up, you can search using their account number or the phone number in their file. If they don't know their account number or phone number, then they need to find it and call back. This is all in the call script."

The man hands me a stack of paper streaked with black marks from a copier. I gently place the papers in my lap.

"Everything you need to know for this job is in those sheets of paper. See, I told you that you didn't need a brain for this job, sweetie," he says with a grin.

I find myself staring over the man's shoulder. I can almost make out people dancing in the cracked wallpaper.

"To be honest, I generally don't like hiring women, since they tend to be more emotional. Always a bit too sensitive to handle the customers who call in yelling, but we've lost so much staff in these past few weeks."

"But you look tough," the yellowed man continues. "You won't wimp out on me, will you darling?"

Not if I want to make rent. I shake my head.

"Now read through those scripts and bring back these forms signed," he passes several sheets of coffee-stained papers, "and get here promptly at 9:50 tomorrow night."

Mr. Richards stands and extends his meaty hand. I rise and tuck the papers

52

under my arm. I delicately place my hand in his claw. The deal is made. I can count on making $72 each night, before taxes.

The cool breeze hits my face as I leave the building. My shoulders release and droop. I am relieved to be out of the building. Thoughts of washing the grease from my body cross my mind, as well as getting my last peaceful night of sleep.

Chapter 2

Sunlight streams into my bedroom through the blinds in stripes of various sizes. Pushing my comforter down, I sit up and look for my phone. It is 10:13 in the morning. A loud crash comes from behind my bedroom wall. My neighbors are fighting again. You can't expect quality neighbors when you choose the cheapest possible apartment.

The photos online for the apartment weren't bad. The interiors were recently refinished. Unfortunately, they used cheap materials done up to look like hardwood and granite. A facade meant to look modern. At least everything is new and I have the one bedroom to myself.

The outside of the apartment is much worse. Each squat two-story building resembles a motel. There are four apartments on the first floor and four apartments on the second floor. Each is identical in size and shape. All are facing the parking lot. The windows and doors are interspaced in the same pattern. Small strips of grass and concrete walkways separate the desolate structures. But rent is only $800 a month. Paying for my online classes is hard enough, especially since I only found a job yesterday.

"OH, NOW YOU'RE GOING TO GO AND DO THAT!" a voice screams past the wall.

"WHAT ARE YOU GOING TO FUCKING DO ABOUT THAT?" retorts a second voice.

At least I don't have roommates. It's just me, Mrs. Can't-keep-her-voice-down, and Mr. Screams-like-he-doesn't-share-a-wall-with-someone.

53

Since I am up, I will get started on my classwork. I fill a bowl with cereal and milk before starting the coffee pot.

Nearby, a door slams.

"WHERE DO YOU THINK YOU ARE GOING?" screams our missus from the parking lot.

"AWAY FROM YOUR BITCH ASS."

"OH, RUN AWAY FROM YOUR PROBLEMS LIKE ALWAYS. MAN UP YOU LITTLE BITCH."

A car screeches away and the door slams again. I can finally study in peace, but he'll probably be back before I return from work. I never understand how they can apologize and move on after such outbursts. I never hear their apologies, so they must be less theatrical than their fights.

I open my laptop and check the assignment list for my Abnormal Psychology class. I need to read chapter 7 and write a paragraph discussion post about it. Afterward, I need to respond to two classmates' discussion posts. An easy assignment.

I have always found psychology interesting. I spend so much time in my own head that I often wonder what it's like for others. From studying psychology, I've learned that our worldviews are shaped by experience. Perception allows us to experience the world around us. But our perception depends on our biology. And our biology can get it wrong. A lack of chemicals in one part of the brain or too many in another and you're functionally abnormal. Too few chemicals make people completely numb to the world around them. Too many chemicals make people believe things that don't make sense, hear things that aren't real, or see things that aren't there.

That isn't to say that these chemicals run everything. Experience comes into play too. Put a sane individual in a bad enough situation and they'll crack. Sanity is like a cup of water. Everyone has a cup. Our biology and brain chemistry decide the size and shape of our cup. Some cups hold more water and some cups may only hold a thimble. Some cups may even come with water in them. Experience fills and empties the cups. Support and healthy coping mechanisms can empty our cups. Bad experiences can fill them. Enough bad experiences will overflow all cups, regardless of size.

Insanity is the water spilling out, dripping down the sides, and puddling the ground around it.

Chapter 3

Industrial street lights keep the darkness at bay as I cross the parking lot. I check my phone for the time. It is only 9:40 PM. I have ten minutes to reach Mr. Richard's office. That should be plenty of time. As I pull the exterior doors open, I notice the elevator doors across the lobby close. As I walk over to the dual elevators, my footsteps click against the marble floor and echo through the empty lobby. Seconds after pressing the call button, the left elevator opens. Stepping inside, I press the plastic button for the 7th floor. I lean against the back wall as the elevator ascends.

When I reach the 7th floor, I know to make a right instead of the left I initially took yesterday. It is much easier to find Mr. Richard's office tonight. The door is already open. The man inside looks up as I reach the doorway.

"I thought I told you to get here at 9:40."

I can't stop from frowning. I just got here and he already has something to gripe about.

"You said 9:50, sir."

He shakes his head. "Regardless, it's 9:55."

9:55? How can it be 9:55? It didn't take fifteen minutes to ride the elevator. I pull out my phone. Sure enough, it is 9:55. Where did that time go?

"Let me show you where you'll be working." Mr. Richards pulls himself up from the chair.

He walks down the hall laboriously. I can almost imagine mud dripping off of him. Mr. Richards opens the door to 2750 and with a flourish of his hands invites me in. Rows of identical cubicles sit under fluorescent lighting. Each desk is set up identically, with a monitor, keyboard, mouse, office phone, and a thin headset. There are no windows.

The room isn't empty. Three young men are dispersed among the desks. Two stare ahead at their monitors, their muscles frozen in place. The last flips through his script. He speaks into his headset and pauses. Then his fingers clatter across the keyboard. His pattern of flipping, speaking, and typing is the only sound outside of the buzzing lights.

"Pick a seat, any seat." Mr. Richards gestures across the nearly empty room.

I select a desk near the man taking the call. He at least seems lively. The stillness of the others makes me feel uneasy.

"Do you have your script?" Mr. Richards asks.

I dig through my bag and pull out a stack of paper. Peeling several sheets off the top, I pass the completed forms to Mr. Richards.

"Here is the paperwork you asked for yesterday."

"Good, good." Mr. Richards nods. "If you have any questions, you can ask Sean before he leaves." He points to the man on the phone before turning and leaving the room.

Sean finishes his call and starts to pack up. One of the statues across the room also makes a motion to grab his bag.

"Don't worry, new girl, it's not that bad," Sean breaks the silence. "You only ever get a few calls this late, right Ken?"

The last statue turns around and replies, "Yeah, and it's generally just problems with pornos. Be sure to bookmark pornography in your script."

"Remember to keep your script out on your desk," Sean continues. "But when it's quiet, you can generally read, do homework, or stream something. When you hear Mr. Richards coming, put whatever you were doing away. He wants to make sure that we are always available to take a call. But he'll leave pretty soon anyway. He doesn't stick around for the night shift."

So, the statues were putting on a show for Mr. Richards's benefit. I would have to follow their example.

"And if you see Ken fall asleep, crumble up some paper and hit him in the head."

Ken smirks. "I'll do the same for you. As a heads up, I generally take my break at 2. You can have 2:30."

I nod.

"Great, you'll do great." Sean gives me a thumbs-up as he departs.

Ken turns back around. He pulls a phone out of his bag and starts watching a video.

This isn't so bad. You just have to exist here until something happens. I can do that. I pull a book from my bag. Settling into my seat, I open at my bookmark.

Sixty pages later, the monitor flashes, notifying an incoming call. The phone rings and I answer, "Thank you for calling Masterson Cable. How can I help you?"

Information linked to the number populates the screen. I scroll through it. The caller lives in the same apartment building as me.

"Yeah, I ordered this movie and it's not very good," a male voice replies. "It's not worth $14.99."

I flip through my script, trying to find the right prompt. "I'm sorry sir, but all sales are final."

"That's stupid," frustration saturates his voice. "Is there a manager I can speak to?"

I flip through the script again. "I'm sorry sir, but to speak to a manager, you will need to call back during business hours, which are 8 AM to 5 PM."

"So there is no one there now that can help me?"

"I'm sorry sir, but to speak to a manager you will have to call back tomorrow after 8 AM but before 5 PM."

"Stupid bitch," he exhales before ending the call with a click.

I sigh. Well, the worst they can do is insult me. I pick up my book and continue reading. As the night draws on, I spend longer staring at each page. The words jumble together and it is harder to concentrate my focus.

Ken sits his phone against his monitor. One earbud trails from Ken to the phone. I can't tell if Ken is trying to be absorbed by the episode or mentally counting the minutes until 2 AM.

It becomes harder to keep my eyes open. Silence fills the room like a blanket. The fluorescent lights and their buzzing fade past consciousness. I can barely perceive them.

I shake my head to try to bring back my stream of thought. Water might help wake me up. I take a long drag from my bottle. I hold the water in my mouth long enough to savor its coolness before swallowing.

I will need to bring an energy drink tomorrow and maybe a movie as well. Staying awake this late is harder than I thought.

I try to return to my book, but the thoughts in my head begin to empty again. My body sinks into the chair. Slowly the edges of my body fade and flow through the chair and into the room. Ken stands up and I snap back.

"Be back in thirty." He waves and walks out carrying his meal.

I nod. Once Ken's footsteps fade, I have to give my face a few light slaps. I'm falling asleep. I should try moving. To stave off sleep, I stand behind my chair. Raising my arms up and to the side, I stretch my lethargic muscles. Before I can feel satisfied with my stretching, the monitor flashes.

It is the same customer as before. I groan before taking the call.

"Thank you for calling Masterson Cable. How can I help you?"

"Help us? Help us? Apparently, you can't do a damned thing," a female voice gripes.

"Leave it alone," the earlier voice interjects in the background.

"No, I'm going to fix this because you aren't enough of a man to do it!"

I recognize the stream of verbal abuse. It is my neighbors.

"You let this little girl on the phone walk all over you," the female voice on the phone continues. "Well, I'll go ahead and tell you that she wants nothing to do with your ass."

"LEAVE IT ALONE!" he screams.

"Not until I tell this little girl what's up."

I hear the phone fumble, followed by indiscriminate yelling. The phone is briefly picked up again before the call ends with a crash. Well, I am awake now.

I shake with anger. My god, how I hate them! They're always yelling. They're always so hateful. I want to say something to them directly, but not after what happened to the last person. The last person that knocked on their door had to face their combined wrath. Their screams featured both expletives and threats. Later, when someone sent a police officer to reign in their behavior, a floodgate of hatred opened. They went on a destructive spree. They scratched threats into cars and threw glass bottles at apartments. They even broke someone's window. The apartment complex advertised

58

security cameras, but the cameras were useless. And no one would take us at our word alone. No pictures of the couple committing their vandalism meant that there was no proof. Mere speculation wasn't enough to get the couple from hell out of the complex. Now everyone did their best to ignore them. Earning their ire wasn't worth it. And yet, I couldn't avoid them in my home and I couldn't avoid them at work. They plagued me like a pest infestation.

I hear footsteps coming down the hall. Ken appears in the doorway.

"You really should take a walk during your break. It will help keep you awake. You just have to get over how creepy an empty office is."

Chapter 4

When I get home at 7 AM, I fall straight into my bed. Sleep takes me before my head hits the pillow. The screech of my alarm at 12:30 is an unwelcome one. My body has not recovered from staying up all night. My head is heavy. My muscles are reluctant. I have only 15 minutes before my online lecture starts. Just enough time to brew some coffee and take a quick shower.

After turning on my coffee maker, I step into my hot shower. My muscles relax as the oils from the previous day slide down my skin. The last of the soap suds are washing down the drain as my coffee maker beeps. The smell of coffee teases me as I get dressed. I throw on sweatpants and a t-shirt and quickly brush through my wet hair before pulling it back.

Dressed and coffee in hand, I make my way to my desk. The desk is pushed up to one of the only two windows in my apartment. Opening the blinds floods the room with fresh light. Unfortunately, the view from my window is of the parking lot.

At 12:44, I flip open my laptop and log into my lecture. For this class, participation counts for 10% of my final grade. The professor asks five poll questions throughout each class meeting. To get full credit for the day, I have to answer all the questions. This professor uses an anonymous poll, which I prefer. I hate answering questions in front of the class. It takes time to put everything together to form a complete answer, but no one will wait for you to think. And when you're slow to answer, people assume you're stupid. And that you don't belong there. I don't want people to assume I'm dumb because of one question. These anonymous polls are much better.

I click through the first question. Correct. The professor moves on. I sink into my seat. Despite the bright light and coffee, exhaustion sits behind my eyelids. I almost miss the second question.

Movement outside my window catches my eye. Five people are walking through the parking lot. The funny thing is that they are all identically dressed. All five are wearing poofy white shirts tucked into brown pants. Their clothes look antiquated and rough. They walk in a straight line into the woods.

I hear my professor mention question three. This one is tough. I select an answer at random. When I look up, the people are gone. The woods past the parking lot aren't dense and my window gives me a perfect view of the direction they are heading. But now, the scene is empty. Exhaustion must be clouding my mind.

I bring my coffee mug to my lips, but the mug has already been drained. My professor drones on. I try to keep my attention focused on the class, but her voice gets flatter. The words merge together. My head nods.

"Final question," my professor's voice snaps through my speakers. I jump awake. Despite missing the question, I attempt an answer.

I snap my laptop shut before looking up. The force of their stares makes me jump backward. Four of the individuals from earlier stand perfectly still at the edge of the woods. All their faces look towards my window. Their hair and shirts drip with water as if they were plunged into a lake. I shut the blinds.

Chapter 5

The drenched people leave me unsettled. I could have sworn I saw five people enter the woods. So why did only four return? And why were they soaking wet? These questions sit in my head without an answer. I don't want to be alone in my apartment after dark, so I bring a couple of books to a local coffee shop. I can order a few coffees and wait for my shift to start. All while listening to the gentle rhythm of light conversation.

I enjoy this shop. The smell of fresh coffee meets each patron at the door. The door is set into a storefront of glass, letting in sunlight or passing headlights. Tables and chairs crowd the floor, windows, and walls. All the furniture is mismatched, but the warm lighting casts a glow across the space. It is a place where things that don't fit in could belong.

The only thing that clouds the comfort of the shop is unpleasant memories. It has been over two months since I last saw Madison. Even so, the heartbreak still pulls melancholic strings in my chest. I can almost picture Madison seated at the table by the window, hunched over a book, her tall and lean frame hidden under a loose dress with caramel hair flowing down her back. As Madison turned the page, the strap of her dress would occasionally slide down her shoulder.

That first night, I was overjoyed that the book Madison was absorbed in was one I knew well. It made it easy to strike up a conversation. As we chatted, we discovered that our similarities were boundless. Over the next few weeks, we visited local coffee shops and hiked through parks together. We enjoyed niche horror movies and shared book recommendations. My feelings for Madison grew stronger. I savored every word Madison uttered. I snatched every opportunity to brush against her skin or hair. I felt the pull of unrequited love.

I catch myself staring at the empty corner table. My thoughts have wandered from my book. Madison is gone. Madison wants nothing to do with me. Checking my watch, I notice that it is time for work.

I try not to dwell on Madison as I walk into the empty office building that night, but the lack of life creates a void. This emptiness brings forth ghosts to fill itself. I am lost in my thoughts. The good memories blend so well with the bad. Madison's harsh rejection bumps against her smile as she cooked. Movies we watched together juxtaposed with being shoved from Madison's apartment. The elevator doors open on the sixth floor.

Stepping out of the elevator, I smell roses. The smell is identical to the lotion that Madison would wear. I used to complain to Madison about my dry hands so she would offer to share her lotion. Taking her signature lotion, I would gently rub it into my hands and arms, savoring the silky feel. For hours afterward, I would relish the scent of roses holding my hands.

The door plate snaps me back to reality. 2617. This is where the call center should be, but the room is empty and unfamiliar. I stare at the plate a moment longer before realizing my mistake. I am on the sixth floor, not the seventh.

I take in my surroundings. There are the same yellowing walls and carpet as the floor above. But this space feels full in its emptiness. It is almost as if I am an intruder in this hallway that savors its few hours without humanity.

A click down the hallway catches my attention. A fluorescent light goes off. The unsettling feeling returns. The hallway is telling me to go away. That I need to leave. So I turn back the way I came. My footsteps fall in a soft thud against the carpet.

Retracing my steps, I quickly find the elevator. I press the up button and nothing happens. The button remains unlit and the elevator is silent. I try again, and again. Then I try down, but the elevator continues to ignore me.

A floorplan above the call button indicates that the stairs are to my right. The lights to my left click off. It seems like I better head right. Anxious, I walk at a brisk pace. I scan the walls and doors hoping to find the stairs, but the signs are meaningless. The numbers don't seem to be in any order. But the lights continue to click off behind me.

The lights prevent me from going back the way I came, but also seem to be leading me deeper into the hallway. I actually crave the fluorescent buzzing of the lighting. Looking into the darkness behind me, I see a shape among the shadows. I want to cry for help, but when the shadow grows into the ceiling, I run instead.

The lights are switching off in loud clunks as large portions of the hallway goes dark. Ahead, one small door remains lit. An exit sign glares in red lettering above the door. I run full force through the door. The stairway is bathed in light. Climbing the stairs two at a time, I only slow down when I reach the door of the call center.

Sitting down at a desk, I check the time. It is only 9:55. I'm not even late. Under the bright lights of the call center, I want to laugh at myself. I was scared by a few shadows. The lights were probably set to go off automatically before 10. And yet, I can't shake how sinister the hallway on the sixth floor felt.

Chapter 6

The blaring of my alarm forces me awake. The harsh sunlight that filters through the blinds disorients me. I roll towards my alarm and my sheets are sticky with sweat. Glimpses of my dreams return to me. I see Madison floating in a pond. She reaches out and asks me to join her. Her subtle movements start a ripple that reaches the end of the water but doesn't stop. It ripples through the ground, kicking up leaves with a crunch. It shakes the trees and knocks me off my feet.

I hate how often my thoughts return to her. I know that we shouldn't be together. She wants nothing to do with me. She told me so. And she has proven it too, as I haven't seen nor heard from her in weeks. It was a dumb idea to try to move beyond friends, but it was so hard to keep my feelings bottled up.

Her body was seated against mine as we shared a blanket on movie night. As the credits rolled, her face turned towards mine, her large eyes gray in the dim lights, like two moons stolen from the sky. I closed my eyes and leaned my face closer to hers, waiting to meet her soft lips. But pain crossed my cheek, forcing my eyes open. Madison's soft features had hardened. Each cruelty she flung cut into my chest. Abomination. False friend. User.

I acted based on emotion, not thought. Even now, my heartbreak feels so raw, like a strip of flesh has been ripped from my torso. But I still hope Madison has a change of heart.

I finally pull myself from my bed. Fresh tears lay against my pillowcase. Opening my blinds in full, I catch my neighbors leaving their apartment. Hand-in-hand, in matching white shirts and brown pants, they head towards the woods. Exchanging smiles, their faces are void of the anger I have come to expect.

That is weird. I consider following them, but I decide to leave them alone. It is better not to get involved with them. I do not want to end up on the receiving end of their wrath. Besides, I am covered in sweat and tears. I opt for a shower instead.

Feeling better after the hot shower, I sit down at my desk with a cup of coffee. I open my sociology textbook. Today's chapter is about the role of society in suicide. The first paragraphs detail the infectious nature of suicide. Whenever a popular star or well-loved student kills themselves, others follow suit.

The book goes on to discuss personal freedom and suicide. Personal freedom exists on a spectrum. When freedom is limited, people may be unable to make choices for themselves. They may not be able to choose their occupations, hobbies, spouses, and relationships. Individuals with limited control over their lives are more likely to kill themselves. Sometimes lack of personal control looks like having someone tell you what to do, but not always. Sometimes people find themselves in a box. A box where they force themselves up in the morning and sit through the same traffic to work the same job. They return home to make dinner, care for children, and clean the day's filth. They lay their heads on their pillows to look forward to the same thing the next day. A life as hopeless as that and I might off myself too.

The opposite end of the spectrum isn't great either. Letting individuals do anything they want can create empty people. People can go to extremes to feel something if they are able to feel anything at all.

But those that survive often find a purpose, something to give meaning to suffering. Something to spend idle time working towards. Something to look forward to during difficult times. What is my purpose? For now, I guess it's to survive long enough to finish school. School won't last forever, and things will be better once I have my degree.

The wind ripples through the trees outside my window. A few leaves are picked up, making turns and swirls like a couple dancing. Through the woods, I make out a figure approaching. As he gets closer, I see that he is my neighbor in the same outfit as before, but he is completely soaked. His clothes are sagging with the weight of the water. He wears the same smile, but he is returning alone.

What is going on? The fall weather isn't freezing, but walking in wet clothes can't be comfortable. I haven't walked around the woods near my apartment, so I don't know what's out there, but perhaps now is the time. Turning down the page before closing my textbook, I resolve to see what is out there.

I wait for my neighbor to get back into his apartment before heading out myself. Slowly opening the door, I make sure that no one is around when I leave my apartment. I head briskly to the woods. A thick layer of leaves coat the ground. The crunching of my footsteps and the wind moving past the leaves are the only sounds in this void. There isn't a clear path, but I see where the leaves have been pressed by footsteps. I follow the impressions. My eyes scan all directions to ensure that I am alone.

After walking for a few minutes, I find a small dark brown pond. Thick mud borders the pond and I can make out several footprints in the mud. I hear the whir of a passing car. Looking up, I see a highway beyond the tree line. It's the highway I take home. I've never noticed this pond on my drive home, but I also don't spend a lot of time looking into the trees as I am driving.

Both my neighbors came into the woods, but only he returned. Perhaps she took the highway into town. That is probably what happened. She might have needed to pick something up at the store. Yet, I can't stop thinking of her drenched at the bottom of the pond.

Chapter 7

I walk into the building with purpose. I am not going to end up on the wrong floor today. I am not going to be late. When the elevator stops, I double-check the floor twice before stepping off. My face moves back and forth as I scan the room numbers. My sigh of relief is audible when I enter the call center.

I nod at Sean before sinking into my seat. He is the only one there. I am pulling a textbook from my bag when Mr. Richards bursts through the open door.

"Jordan."

At the sound of my name, my head snaps up to face Mr. Richards.

"Ken won't make it tonight, so you're alone. There won't be a meal break tonight. Keep your bathroom breaks short. The phone will keep ringing until you pick it up. Don't keep them waiting too long. I can check the logs tomorrow and see how long the phone was ringing."

"I won't keep them waiting, sir," I respond, hoping to placate Mr. Richards.

"Good." He raps his hands against the door frame twice before leaving.

I don't like the idea of being alone tonight. Looking at my desk, I feel the compulsion to take a sip of my water. The cool liquid slides down my throat and calms my nerves. Opening my textbook, I dive into the content as Sean packs up and leaves.

After reading each section, I diligently write down the main idea of the text. I also write down each vocabulary word with its definition. Each time my mind drifts away, I recalibrate. I re-read the sentences I glazed over. Almost unconsciously, I keep reaching for my water to take a sip.

Later into the night of uninterrupted study, I try to take a sip of water, but my lips remain dry. My bottle is empty. I also realize that I need to use the restroom. Closing my textbook, I walk into the hall.

The blaring lights buzz. I first stop at the water fountain. The clear water splashes and gurgles into the bottle. I cannot resist leaning down into the water's spray and filling my mouth.

I step into the bathroom and my footsteps smack into standing water. The water is just deep enough to cover the grungy tile floor. Is there a leak? Looking under the sinks and behind the toilets, I can't find anything. Everything else in the bathroom is dry. Perhaps someone on an earlier shift had been playing around in the sinks. I could see an annoyed employee taking out their frustrations by flooding the sinks.

Since nothing is actively leaking, I decide to leave the water for now. I don't think it is a huge problem. Besides, who could I tell? Mr. Richards never gave me a number. I don't even know how to find the number for building maintenance. I decide to leave a note on Mr. Richard's door and call it a day.

Walking into the first stall, I close the door behind me. I sit and relieve myself. As I finish, I hear the smacking of footsteps against the water.

"Hello. Is someone there?" I ask.

The footsteps continue. Smack. Smack. Smack. Pacing by the sink, the footsteps are speeding up, each step smacking the water like a drum. SMACK SMACK SMACK. I stand and open the stall door. There is a heavy silence. Looking at the sink, I see nothing besides the water.

That is weird. I hope this place doesn't have rats. I shiver at the thought. After washing my hands, I check for leaking water again. Finding none, I step into the hallway.

The faint sound of a phone ringing bounces across the walls. I curse myself for spending so long in the bathroom. As I jog back to the call center, I try to calculate how long the phone could have been ringing.

Throwing myself into my seat, I grab the headset and pick up the call. It is my neighbor calling again. Groaning, I prepare for the worst.

"Thank you for calling Masterson Cable. How can I help you?" My voice comes across as sickishly cheery. I have mastered the customer service voice.

No response comes. I wait.

"Hello? Are you there? You've reached Masterson Cable. Can I help you?"

Across the line, water is shifting.

"You want to know how to help me?" a flat female voice answers, sliding down my headpiece like honey. "That's funny. I called to help you."

"How so?" I am drawn in.

"You are so stressed, my dear. You are worn out. Tired. Stretched thin. You are doing too much because you think you have no other option."

The speaker slowly pronounces each word. The effect bathes me in serenity. My head aches from exhaustion. I can't hold a thought beyond the speaker's voice.

"You do have a choice. I know because I was just like you. And now, I have been led to my salvation. I have come back to lead you."

Water splashes behind the voice.

"It's so simple," the speaker continues, "water is our salvation. It was never dust to dust. We are not creatures of dust. We are creatures of water. Water to water. We must return to the water."

"Water?" I question.

"Yes, water." The speaker quickens her speech and raises her voice, like a preacher reaching his point. "Water is salvation and you must seek it. WATER TO WATER. WE MUST RETURN TO WATER. YOU WILL BE RETURNED TO THE WATER. YOU WILL BE DRENCHED," the voice is yelling now.

The hypnosis is broken. I click the mouse to disconnect the call. Alone, I finally notice how heavily I am breathing. Taking off the headset, I feel a drop of sweat drip down my ear. My agitation does not diminish as I wait for morning.

Chapter 8

That call was disturbing. I still feel on edge. My muscles are tense as if I have stepped up to the starting line. Lying in bed, I beg for sleep. My head is so heavy. My thoughts are fuzzy. Frustrated tears cross my cheeks. I just want to sleep. But sleep isn't coming at this rate. I throw off my comforter.

Perhaps a bath and a drink would help. I leave the lights off, opting to light a few candles instead. I uncork a cheap bottle of wine and decide not to bother with a glass. The rush of water into the tub fills my head. Sipping on the wine, I slide into the tub. By the time the tub is full, half the wine is gone. I shut off the water with a click and am met with silence except for the occasional crackle from the candle's wick.

The heat digs into my muscles like fingers. My legs, my arms, my back, and my neck loosen. I stare into the corner of my tub. I notice black cracks between my tub and the wall. I've never noticed the cracks before. Are they new? I try not to imagine long spindly fingers pulling the cracks open. I try not to think about small bugs crawling through the cracks. I push away thoughts of tiny insects pressing against each other as they strive to break through. I try to shake off these thoughts and focus on something else.

Warm water envelops my arms and shoulders. I sink deeper into the water and feel its embrace. My eyelids fall and I am unable to resist sleep. I am falling. The bottom of the tub drops from under me. My head splashes into the water as my body sinks deeper. I throw my arms out. My fingers search for the edge of the tub but only find water. I push my feet downwards and begin kicking up. In a few kicks, my head breaks the water's surface.

I gasp for air and fill my lungs. Cicadas sing around me. The sky is dark, but I can see streetlamps and passing headlights through the trees. I head towards the lights. I need to get out of this water.

"You are not cleansed yet," a voice under me calls. Hands grab my waist and pull me down.

I sit up gasping. My hands grasp the edge of the tub. I had fallen asleep. It was just a dream. And yet, I am on edge. My heart is thumping against my chest. The air tastes sour. My candles went out and the light is thin.

How long was I asleep? I wrap a towel around myself and look for my phone. 9:30 PM. I freeze as I think of the consequences. I have been asleep all day. And I am going to be late for work.

Anxious thoughts fill my head. I am going to be late. I could get fired. Could I find another job that didn't cut into my class time? Would that job allow me to do homework in my downtime, even secretly? Would I have enough money to make rent? Running through my apartment, I pull on clothes. I pull back my hair, throw my homework and some food into my bag, and run out the door.

Chapter 9

I drive erratically to work. I speed around cars and merely glance before making turns. But it is only 9:50 when I enter the parking lot. My anxiety is high, but I might be able to slide in unnoticed.

My footsteps reverberate through the empty lobby. Each click against the floor echoes the heartbeat in my head. As I approach the elevators, the doors slide open with a cheerful ding. I plow into the elevator. I am running on adrenaline. I jab the button for the 7th floor and the elevator ascends.

Impatiently, I pace in the elevator. The numbers above me light and dim in sequence. 2 . . . 3 . . . 4 . . . 5 . . . 6. The doors open and I dart out. Gripping my bag close to my body, I run. I keep my footsteps light to avoid suspicion as I round the corners of the hallways.

Upon the last turn, I slow to a fast walk. Gripping the door to the call center, I gingerly pull it open to find a bathroom. My face falls. I am on the sixth floor. I got off on the wrong floor, again. I pull my phone out to check the time. 11:58 PM.

That makes no sense. I try to open my phone's web browser to confirm the time, but I don't have service. Still standing in the bathroom, I turn to leave. A splashing sound catches my attention.

"Who's there?" I ask.

Two shoes step down in a stall, splashing the water that covered the bathroom floor.

"Hello?" My voice cuts through the bathroom.

The shoes squeak as the wearer's weight shifts. As they stand, water drips down onto the floor from their clothing. The droplets continue to fall as they step to the stall door and pull back the lock.

The bathroom door slams behind me as I run down the hall. My footsteps squish into the carpet. I look down at the floor. The carpet is wet too. I see the exit sign from earlier.

"The stairs!" I exclaim.

I burst through the door below the exit sign and run straight into standing water. My feet are immediately drenched. It must be six inches deep.

Standing still now, I look around the room. This isn't the stairs. This is another bathroom. Something splashes in the corner.

"You're so worried," a smooth voice calls out. "You're so anxious. We have just the solution for that."

"And what's that?" I reply.

"The water provides everything you need, honey. You don't have to work or study for the water. The water accepts you as you are. You are never late for the water. The water will wait for as long as it takes. Because you will return to the water. YOU BELONG TO THE WATER."

A hand emerges from the puddled water and grips my ankle. I kick at the hand as it tries to pull me off balance. The hand releases me and I run from the bathroom.

Elevator, elevator, where is the elevator? My mind races. I look around each corner, but each turn only offers hallways. Hallways with yellowing paint, fluorescent lighting, and wet, gray carpets. Hallways lined with identical doors.

I sprint down the hallways, looking at each door for a number, but each door says the same thing: Water. Every turn. Every hallway. Every door. Water. Water. Water.

I have been running for miles. I stop to pull out my phone and catch my breath. I have no service. It is 11:58.

"No," I squeak out.

"What do I do?" I groan.

"Don't do anything," the voice like honey answers me. A calm voice. A confident voice.

Down the hallway, an overhead light clicks off. Another click and another light is off. In the darkened hallway, I make out a figure.

"I won't hurt you," the figure offers. "You will never hurt again."

Shaking my head, I turn to run.

"No, I can't give up. I need to keep fighting," I tell myself.

"You've tried for so long," the figure answers. "Trying is so hard. Accepting us is the path forward."

I am panting. I am exhausted. An aching fills my chest.

"Why not have a seat here?" The figure gestures towards the wall.

My body cries out for rest. I feel immediate relief as I sit down. The water is deeper now. It flows around me tenderly. I rest my head in my hands.

"You are tired. Why don't you rest?"

The water gurgles. The sound eases the tension in my head. Relaxing my jaw, I sink deeper into my hands. The water lays upon me like a blanket. It gently massages my muscles.

"Doesn't it feel nice?" the figure whispers into my ear.

My heavy eyelids fall closed. The figure softly lays me down into the water.

"You'll feel so much better now. Nothing solves your problems like being drenched."

The water pushes my hair back and forth. I open my eyes to see little bubbles emerge from my face and float upwards. The flowing water caresses my arms and legs. I am finally at peace.

Under the Cover of Darkness

The destroyer of our world fell from the sky. He came as a dazzling light from the heavens. I sometimes imagine that he came from a thoughtless wish made upon a shooting star. A wish made by a madman cursing us all or an upset child unaware of the power behind his words. Looking up to the heavens and seeing that falling light, they uttered, "I wish everyone was gone." If it was a wish gone wrong, then I could undo it. I could wish that everything was back to normal and it would be like this never happened. I would save the day and we would all be happy again. Then my suffering would have a purpose. Because otherwise, why am I still here?

A small flaming rock fell from the sky and brought with it our destruction. The rock was really quite small, and yet, it brought a monster to Earth. The monster had no form. He could have passed through us unnoticed and undetected if not for his voice. He had a strong, clear voice. He would use his voice to lure, entice, and cajole people to their deaths, as if our lives were just a game.

Our destruction came so quickly. As the daylight faded into dusk, I saw the bright light flash across the sky. My feet froze in place as my eyes tracked the falling ball of the flame's descent. After it passed my line of sight, I noticed that everyone around me had stopped as well. We shared confused glances as questions formed on our lips.

The ground beneath us rocked as the meteor made an impact. Dozens of eyes were glued in the direction of the falling star. And then, the screaming began. A wave of people fled from the meteor's direction. They seemingly ran from nothing. My feet were not convinced to flee, so I remained in place.

My mind changed when I saw bodies crumble. They flew through the air like papers being tossed into a wastebasket.

I was lucky. I stood next to a movie theater. I ran in shouting to the staff that a monster was outside. I entreated them to hide or run, but their eyes demanded proof. I ran into one of the theaters, screaming my warning over the featured film. But like Cassandra, my warning would go unheeded.

Louder than my own and devoid of emotion, a smooth voice from the lobby countered, "There is a madwoman in the theater. Make your way to the lobby for your own safety."

Behind me, the movie continued. The theater patrons shifted their eyes between me, the screen, and the exit doors. Finally, the projector clicked off, leaving us in the theater under the cover of darkness.

"Come into the lobby for your own safety," the voice boomed.

I watched in horror as everyone began to stand and walk towards the exit.

"No!" I screamed. I pleaded, "Don't head towards him! Hide! Run away! He'll kill you."

But they ignored me or shook their heads. I ran up to a young woman and tried to pull her away, but she resisted. Her fingers tried to pry mine off. There was fear in her features, but it was directed towards me. To escape my grip, she shoved me to the floor. She ran out the door and I was alone in the theater.

"Don't you want to come out, too?" the voice asked from the lobby.

I hid under a chair near the emergency exit.

"I know you're still in there."

Behind the theater doors, the lobby erupted in tortured screaming and the crunching of bones.

"You can't hide from me forever, but I have better things to attend to," were the last utterances from the voice before silence fell.

I sat in my hiding spot like a tree rooted in place. At first, I expected him to sneak into the theater. I thought he was trying to trick me by pretending to leave. I was an insect living under a rock, prepared to scurry away once the stone was removed. But as the hours passed, I wondered why the ax never fell.

Sleep fell so gently upon me that I only realized I had fallen asleep when I woke up, pressed against the side of the seat. I was still alive, but how much time had passed? Eventually, hunger and thirst pulled me from my position. Slowly, to limit noise, I searched the rows of seats. Within a few steps, I found flat soda, cold popcorn, and sticky candy. My hunger satiated, I continued to hide.

It's hard to say how much time passed as I sat there in the dark. I was stolen by sleep several times. I scoured every seat for forgotten snacks, relieved myself in emptied cups, and waited for death that never came.

The images of the falling star and crumbled bodies replayed in my mind to the soundtrack of his voice. Why didn't he come into the theater to kill me when he had the chance? His ability to destroy lives and toss a person led me to believe that he was physically quite strong. But he didn't kill me. In fact, he didn't hurt anyone while they were sitting in the dark theater. He persuaded them to enter the lit lobby first. What if he was afraid of the dark? I nearly chuckled at the thought, but as I sat alone in shadow, the idea gained traction. He was afraid of the dark. To survive, I needed to stay within the darkness.

Eventually, the lights in the lobby clicked off. The yellow fluorescent line from under the door disappeared. Did this mean there was no one left to man the power stations? Was my city out of power? Could I even think of rescue? I imagined the streets, shops, and workplaces empty. But that wouldn't be right. They would be filled with dead bodies lying on the ground like forgotten dolls.

I couldn't sit here forever. My food was beginning to run out. I thought of the buttered, golden popcorn in the concession stand. With the fluorescent lights off, I judged daytime through the dim light from under the theater door. I waited until the line disappeared before I slowly opened the door to the lobby. The smell of rotting flesh struck me like a slap to the face. I gagged. My hands clasped over my mouth and nostrils, holding back the sound of my disgust as well as shielding the smell.

I waited with the door partially open, letting myself adjust to the smell. The bodies on the floor came into focus as well as the edges of the concession stand and ticket booth. Slowly, I took a step, letting one foot cross the threshold of the door before the other foot followed.

I gently closed the door behind me. Timid step by timid step, I maneuvered around the lumps of flesh on the floor. The night was silent, allowing even my most gentle steps to pierce the void. I eventually made it behind the counter. I looked into the popcorn maker and saw wriggling insects. The view turned my stomach. I searched under the counter. I was rewarded with stacked candy boxes and orderly rows of water bottles. I found bags of chips and stacks of napkins. There were several trips to take this bounty back into the safety of the theater.

Over the next few days, I planned. I thought of the nearby stores. I could find food, cushions, blankets, and warm clothes. There should be whatever I needed to survive and make my new home more comfortable without needing light or sound.

A new routine was formed. I slept away the daylight and scavenged during the night. In the space between the seats and screen, I dragged cushions, blankets, and pillows for a bed. The makeshift bed was far more comfortable than the floor. I even found a gas camping stove to cook the canned food I found. A bucket set near the door served as my bathroom, which I emptied each night.

One nightfall, I even dressed in trash bags and dragged the bodies from the lobby to another theater. Out of sight, out of mind. Well, at least they wouldn't be a tripping hazard.

I tried to keep my trips out of the theater short, which gave me a lot of time to sit and think. Initially, this gave me plenty of time to plan my supply trips. But as I became more physically comfortable, I was haunted mentally. There was nothing to distract myself from my thoughts. While my eyes had adjusted enough to navigate in the dark, I was unable to pick out letters on a page. Books were meaningless objects. Even if I could get electricity for a tablet or laptop, I feared the light it emitted. I feared all light and sound, lest it should give me away.

I became a creature of darkness. Shying away from the light, I moved silently between dark corners. The dark and quiet shielded me from certain death, but what sort of life did I lead? I fear my humanity slipped away as my skin tightened and faded to alabaster and my eyes widened to capture meager moonlight. Would I look more like a living statue or a monster myself?

Oh, how I missed the sunlight! I craved its warmth upon my skin. I ached to see the splendor and beauty of a sun-dappled path or a bright square, where people chat over the songs of birds and insects. I imagined myself walking through lush forests, colorful gardens, and city blocks. I held images in my mind of green trees standing tall and gently swaying in the wind, delicate flower petals and their soft scent, and smiling passersby. But everything felt false when imagined from darkness.

To be alone in the quiet darkness grew maddening. I thought of the shooting star. I made my own wish upon its memory to return to normalcy. But I also thought of others like me, hiding in the darkness. I held hope that I wasn't alone, which gave me the courage to take action.

Filling a backpack with supplies, I began my journey. I traveled only at night and slept in windowless rooms deep within buildings and underground in sewers. Rot was everywhere. Decaying bodies of both animals and people met me on the streets and inside homes. And all around me, the world remained silent. The enormity of it discouraged me. It was hard to keep hope while surrounded by this much death. With each body, I would look towards the sky searching for a shooting star.

But none appeared. No shooting stars. No signs of life. I walked for months, across states, but the only thing I ever found was the darkness, the quiet, and myself.

I grew lazy. I gravitated towards easier shelters. I spent less time walking each night and more time laying in my sleeping bag staring at nothing. I considered giving up. As I fell asleep in a small gas station bathroom, I thought of the sun on my skin and of conversations with friends.

I awoke with a start. Fear set in immediately. I must have heard something but what? Was it the front door? My eyes adjusted to the darkness. A strip of sunlight was visible under the bathroom door. It was still daylight. Could it be another person? At long last?

"I know you're in there," a voice called from beyond the door. His voice. "I can hear your heartbeat from here."

Stupid, stupid, stupid! This was the stupidest place to sleep! Once he opened the door, this entire bathroom would be flooded with daylight. I ran to the door and pressed my weight against it. It wouldn't be enough to keep him out, but what other option did I have?

"I don't want to hurt you," his voice was pressed to the other side of the door. "I've killed everything else on this planet. There is nothing else. But I see now how that was a mistake. I am alone and I've been alone for so long. I don't want to be alone any longer. Please come out. I promise I won't hurt you."

"I don't believe you!" I shouted into the door. "I've seen your aftermath. You're nothing but a monster!"

It was so hard to maintain my facade of strength when my body was shaking so much.

"You're right," he sounded almost remorseful. "I was wrong. It was a mistake. I didn't know better at the time, but now I do. I don't want to be alone. Please don't leave me alone."

He began to push on the door. I knew I couldn't hold him back forever, but I could trap him in the dark with me. I could hurt him just a little before he killed me. In one swift motion, I pulled the door open wide before slamming it shut. I sat against the door to hold it closed. I heard a sigh within the bathroom and I knew that I was successful. He had fallen into the darkness with me.

"That was a clever trick. You've trapped me in the dark bathroom. But now what?"

I really didn't know. I wasn't even fully expecting my plan to work. And if it did work, I expected to be killed shortly after. But here we were. Together in the darkness.

He sighed again. "I probably deserved this. I really don't like the dark." His voice cracked. "But I think that being alone was worse."

My thoughts were racing. Maybe he was never afraid of the dark. Maybe it was a grand scheme to give me hope of survival before dashing it away. He was cruel and clever after all.

"You aren't speaking to me." He waited for a response that never came. "But

I know you're still here. I can hear you. And you must be alone too."

"I am alone." I held down the growing knot in my throat. Sliding down the length of the door, I sat on the floor.

"Well, we don't have to be. We can have each other. Here, let me try to become more like you."

I wondered if he was toying with me. If so, he knew exactly where to hit me. I was alone. I had fought so hard to survive, but I was tired of trying. The silence was so heavy. The aching in my side cut deeper. The lump in my throat was too dry to swallow. What was the point of survival if it only extended my misery? There was no hope. He'd already admitted to killing everything else. I was ready to die. Accept the end.

"There we go," his voice sounded pleased. I heard someone sliding down the door. Then I felt his arm pressed against mine. "How's that?"

I didn't know what to say. He was a disembodied voice, but now in the dim light, I made out the outline of a person sitting next to me.

"I hope this is better," he tried again. "I hoped that you would like me better if I looked more like you. I know you won't forgive me immediately, but I want to work towards earning your forgiveness."

His fingers interweaved with mine. "The dark isn't so bad when you're not alone," he whispered into my ear.

His hand was warm and rough. Against reason, it felt comforting. With my other hand, I counted his fingers. He had five fingers. I followed his fingers to his hand and up his arm and to his torso. I pulled my hand free from his and let my fingers roam across his face, his shoulders, and his hair. He was a person. The ache in my side opened and I couldn't hold back any longer. I sobbed. Hot tears streamed down my face and my body shook.

He pulled my face into his chest. "It's okay. It's okay. You don't have to be alone any longer. You don't have to hide in the darkness any longer." He gently brushed his fingers through my hair.

"What's your name?" he asked.

"Faith," I whispered into his shoulder. "What should I call you?"

"Felix."

I nodded. Leaving my face on his shoulder, I continued to cry. I cried because I had seen so much death and because I fought so hard to survive. I soaked Felix's shirt with my tears, but I couldn't stop. Water drained from my eyes. My tears could fill an ocean. I cried for myself. I cried for humanity. Felix pressed his face into my hair.

Despite everything, his embrace was comforting. He rubbed my back and I sank further into his body. I cried because I lost. I was done fighting. I was drenched in tears. I was done living in the darkness. I gave up so much to hide from him, to cheat death, but I would throw it all away just to feel like I had a friend.

Additional Story: I Love You to Hell and Back

My husband was a good man once. We were happy together and I loved him then. But as his gambling addiction worsened, our despair grew. We went deeper and deeper into debt to support his compulsion to gamble. I begged him to stop. I pleaded. He lost our home. He wagered away our car. I thought he had nothing left to bet, but I was wrong.

My husband sits before me. His shame is so palpable that it fills the space between us. His head hangs as if an invisible noose circles his neck. Stuttering, he tries to offer an explanation. In a broken speech, my husband claims to have made a bet with the devil. A bet that would have paid off his debts and ensured his financial security. Regardless, it was a bet that he lost. The devil's price for such a potential reward was high. The devil asked that my husband use our children as leverage and my husband agreed.

Worthless man! The children weren't his to bet. He didn't carry their weight within him for months. His organs didn't shift to make room for them. They never tore his flesh as they welcomed the world. I did everything for my children. I sang them to sleep. I eased their pain. I held them in my arms so they could better see the world. I strapped them to my back as I completed chores and errands so that they would never be alone. I listened to childish tales and showed interest in their whims. I sacrificed for these children, while he offered them nothing. The children were mine.

The man sitting before me is dead to me. I can never forgive him. Brianna is only four and Brandon is just six. Brianna and Brandon would dance around me, living in their world of pretend. Together, they would slay dragons, find treasure, rescue princesses, and fight pirates. They remained cheerful even as I worried over finding our next meal. Brianna and Brandon were my lighthouse through choppy waters. And my husband, he didn't care as he dashed the ship to pieces upon the rocky shore.

I won't stand for the loss of my children. My rage sets me in motion. If my husband can wager my children to the devil, I could win them back. I search every seedy bar, dark warehouse, and rundown business. I return to every location where I have found my husband after a bad night. Soon enough, I find the devil.

The devil sits at a wooden table within a dark basement bar. Thick, dark hair is gelled down over his horns. As I reach the last step, the devil smiles at me. Gesturing at the seat in front of him, he invites me to sit.

"I would like to trade my husband for my children in Hell," I say as I take the seat he offers.

He shakes his head while continuing to smile. "I'm afraid it doesn't work like that."

"Why not?"

"Your husband isn't yours to offer."

I scoff. "But he can offer my children?"

"Until they are adults, children are property owned by their parents. Adults own themselves."

I smack the table. "THAT'S BULLSHIT!"

His smile turns into a smirk. "These are my rules. If adults could pawn off the souls of each other, you would already be mine."

The blood drains from my face. "My husband tried to offer me, too?"

The devil nods.

I sit back, deflated. "But what can I do?"

"Well, since you also owned the children, I will offer you the opportunity to get them back."

"How?" I ask too quickly

He pauses before answering. "I will take you through the gates of Hell. I will also give you three passes to get back out of Hell. Once you find your children in Hell, you only need to take them back to the gates and walk out."

"What's the catch?" I question suspiciously.

"There is no catch. Even with the passes, finding your children and getting them back to the gates will be difficult. You will have to pass through all of Hell and back. I don't think you will succeed."

"But, there is a chance I will?"

"Yes, you may be able to save your children."

I sigh. "Then I will take it."

"Then we have a deal." The devil offers his hand and I shake it. "I'll give you a few hours to prepare."

I'm not sure what I'll need in Hell, but I pack some water, food, salt, a stake, and a cross. I hope that will be enough to protect myself from the demons and monsters I find there.

I return to the devil with my pack and he motions for me to follow him. He leads me out of town and through darkened woods. The trees around us stand tall, but the shadows they cast are taller. We don't follow a path, but the devil seems sure of his direction. The trees soon open up to a clearing. He turns back to me and smiles. With the wave of his hands, large iron gates appear before us. Blackness lies beyond the gates.

"We're here," the devil says with a flourish of his hands.

The devil pulls out three gold coins from his pocket and hands them to me. Each is inscribed in a language I cannot read.

"These are your passes. You can walk through the gates as long as you hold one of these."

The gates ease open. Metal clangs and groans. When the opening is wide enough for a person to pass through, the gates stop.

The devil gestures to the opening and Hell beyond. "Good luck."

I walk through the gates and plunge into darkness. The gates swing closed behind me in an abrupt clang. I trudge forward into the sea of black. I wander for hours through this nothingness. This void. This limbo. I walk and I walk and nothing changes. But then, I hear a sound. Someone is crying.

I head towards the noise. No matter how many steps I take, the crying feels so far away. Steadily, the sobbing becomes louder. The darkness fades into a gray dawn. Many hours pass before I find the source of the sound. It's a small child. Long, stringy black hair covers her face. Her dress is in rags. She is so pale that she looks gray.

"What's wrong?" I ask.

She looks up at me, but doesn't respond. Instead, the child continues to cry. Her sobs shake her whole body. I gently rub her back, trying to comfort her. The child does not acknowledge me.

"Can I help you with something?" I place my face next to hers, but she keeps crying.

Squatting to her level, I wrap my arms around the child. Rocking back and forth, I whisper that it will be alright. She continues to weep as if I'm not there.

I try to pick her up, but she is heavier than I can carry. She doesn't budge. That isn't right. The child looks so small and fragile. I try again. My body strains against the weight of the child, but she is rooted in place. Tugging just at her feet, I see that she is connected to the ground. The child cannot leave this spot.

Frustrated tears fall down my cheeks. I cannot help this child. She is stuck here. I hope my children don't face the same fate.

I leave the child. She tugs at my heart, but I don't know what else to do. I carry forward. The light gradually increases and I see the landscape around me. The world is flat, covered in dirt and dotted with rocks. Nothing grows here. Over the horizon, there are small orange orbs. Small fires dot the landscape. I approach one, but I keep my distance.

Around the fire sits a group of people in rags. Their skin is gray and is pulled taunt across their bodies. Bones protrude, except for their bulbous stomachs. The group gleefully feasts on bits of meat they pull from the fire. Blood blackens their fingers and mouths. They don't notice me over their meal

At another fire, screams ring out. A group has overpowered an individual and drags their body over the fire. Fingers tear into the flesh of the body, trying to pull them apart. Their screams fall on deaf ears.

I run away from the fires. I avoid them as I continue forward, leaving a wide berth between them and myself. Like the darkness, the fires fade behind me.

Now groaning permeates the air. It starts low, but gets louder as I approach. I come to the edge of a large pit, hundreds of feet wide and twenty feet deep. Dozens of people are stuck in the pit. Gold and jewels blanket the bottom of the pit, but few rejoice in their riches. Several are trying to clamber up the side, but slide down before progress is made. The sides of the pit are smooth. The people scrambling up the sides of the pit have bloody hands, arms, and feet. Others sit among the jewels nursing broken bones.

"Hey, you!" A voice calls to me from the pit. It is the first time someone has spoken to me in Hell. The speaker is a young man. His hair and beard are shaggy and his clothes are torn. He presses himself against the edge of the pit.

"You at the edge," he yells at me again.

"Yes?"

"Can you throw down a rope?" He asks.

"I don't have a rope. Is there one up here?" I look around me.

"No, you need to go find a rope."

I shake my head. "I don't have time to search for a rope."

"Then reach your arm down here and help lift me up." He commands.

"I'm sorry, but the distance is too great. It wouldn't work."

His voice cracks. "You can't just leave me here."

"I'm sorry, but I need to find my children."

I leave the man looking forlorn up at the pit's edge. My children come first. I need to get them out of Hell. I can't risk ending up in the pit like the others. I walk onward.

The air becomes drier. A chill descends upon my bones. I pull my hands into my shirt and tuck my arms closer. The wind picks up. It whips my hair and bites my exposed skin. A layer of ice coats the ground. Despite the pain, I continue forward.

As I walk, I start to find body parts strewn across the ground. First, it's feet. Then I pass legs, hands, and arms. Pieces of human bodies are frozen to the ground and long forgotten. Finally, I find the torsos. What remains of each person crawls along the ice. Some are missing a leg or a foot. Others are torsos with heads. They never take note of my presence. Their eyes are blank. Yet, something compels them to move forward.

I run. I run out of the icy plane and I don't stop until I feel dirt under me. Time continues to pass. I cannot tell if I have been here for hours or days. I've passed by several hundred people, but none of them resemble my children. Many of them barely resemble people. I've seen the tortured souls that are forced to endure this misery for eternity. But as I think about it, there must be millions of people in hell. So where are they? I must have a lot more ground to cover and much more of Hell to see.

My legs ache and my feet hurt, but I keep moving. I have what many others in Hell lack: Hope. I have as much time as I need to find my children. It doesn't matter if they are deformed, broken, or missing pieces. I will take whatever remains of them back to Earth.

Fog descends upon the ground and shapes emerge through the mist. Gravestones and crypts appear through the haze. This part of Hell is quiet. The fog muffles sound, but a ring of metal against stone occasionally pierces the veil. I head into the graveyard. To my surprise, I see that the ground in front of each grave isn't filled. Within each hole, a person lies uncovered. None of them are rotting. They all look like they are sleeping.

I pass the open graves. Soon, I find an old woman sitting next to an empty pit. Her long gray hair hangs in her face. She holds a hammer and chisel in her mud covered hands to etch a name into a stone. Once her task is complete, she lays her tools aside and climbs into the hole. The old woman lays down, closes her eyes, and invites death.

"What are you doing?" I ask.

She opens one eye and frowns. "Dying. Isn't that obvious?"

"But why?"

"Because I'm supposed to be dead."

"But you are dead."

She sits up and exhales. "I am supposed to be resting. I am supposed to cease my existence. I am supposed to be welcoming the void. Now leave me alone!"

I comply with her final wishes. I pass someone digging a grave, but I leave them alone. This ring of hell exists for the hopeless, but I still carry the flame of hope within me. My mouth is dry and my stomach growls, but I ignore my physical body. What if my children are hungrier or thirstier than I? I will hold off from dipping into my supplies as long as I can for them.

The graves become further apart and a cityscape emerges. Paved, but cracked, streets begin. As I walk, people flit from alleyways and buildings. They never make eye contact. Each looks scared, but of what? I see no monsters here. I tap a woman on the arm as she walks past.

"Excuse me," I try to get her attention.

"What do you want?" The woman throws back.

"I'm looking for my children. Have you seen two children?"

"Children?" Her brow furrows. "Children in Hell are rare."

"They are both young. My daughter is four and my son is six. They have dark hair and big brown eyes."

The woman shakes her head. "Four and six? How did they end up here?"

"Their father bartered them to the Devil and lost," I coldly reply.

The woman looks down. Her expression becomes sympathetic. "I'm sorry to hear that. I hope my children never end up here." She pauses and looks around. Pointing to her right, she continues, "Over there is a large forest. It's where the pedophiles hide. I would recommend looking there."

I thank her before setting off towards the forest. Within the woods, hunched men and women move from tree to tree. They move like prey, alert to each sound and movement. A strange blue thumbprint dots their cheeks.

The sound of a horn echoes through the trees and the marked people react fearfully to the sound. They sprint away from the direction of the horn or hide. A group of people run into the woods following the horn. This group looks like they came from the city. There is nothing to mark them. I stand frozen as the group catches a marked haggard man. In synchrony, the group beats the man with fists. Once the man falls to the ground, they kick him. Soon, the attackers fall to their knees and dig their fingers into the man's flesh, pulling him apart.

I stand transfixed. This group reminds me of the cannibals, but passion and hatred sits behind their eyes, not hunger. If not for their bloody hands, they would look normal. Their clothes are dirty, but intact. After tearing the man apart, they leave what remains of the man and leave.

A voice whispers in my ear and startles me. "Are you new here or something?"

I turn to face the speaker. A man stands behind me. Stubble wraps around his face, but it doesn't hide the blue mark.

"You're unmarked. You don't belong here."

"What do the marks mean?" I ask.

"Wow, you must be new." He points to his face. "The marks mean that we are prey for the hunters."

"The hunters?"

"They hunt us for sport." He gestures to the mound of flesh that was once a man.

"But why?"

The man laughs at my question. "We're in Hell. Why not?"

"What happens after you're killed in Hell?"

The man's face drops. He becomes solemn. His previous laughter dies on his lips. "You never really die in Hell. You're trapped in your body forever, even if you're in pieces."

I don't know what to say. The silence hangs heavy between us. I take a deep breath and change the subject. "I'm looking for two children. A brother and sister, aged six and four."

"What for?" The man asks.

"They're my children."

The man swallows and nods. "And you're certain they're in Hell?"

"Yes."

He sighs. "I've heard a rumor that deep in these woods, there is a madman with two children." The man points away from the city. "Head that way. The trees will get thicker, but keep going. I hope your children are intact when you find them."

I nod and head deeper into the woods. I see fewer and fewer people the further I walk. I hear the horn blare again, but the sound is far off. As the man said, the trees grow thicker. Their branches scratch my face and arms, but I push forward. The light thins and the world becomes shades of gray.

Ahead, I make out orbs of golden light. I walk closer. A cave comes into view with light spilling from the cave's opening. I tentatively walk through the cave's entrance.

The cave opens into a large room. Curtains cover the back, hiding the cave's true size. The room is well furnished. A dark red couch stands in front of a roaring fire. Bookcases line the walls, overflowing with books. In the middle of the room, a well-dressed man sits at a wooden table. He holds a glass of red wine in one hand and holds down the page of an open book in the other. Despite his rapt attention, he looks disinterested in his reading choice.

I take another step into the cave and the man's eyes move from the page to mine.

"Hello." His voice is rich and flows like caramel. "May I help you?"

"I am looking for the madman."

A smile grows from his mouth. He closes his book. "You've found him."

"Do you have my children?"

"Your children? The children here belong to me."

"May I see them?"

"Certainly. BRING THE CHILDREN FORWARD!" He shouts to the curtain.

A crooked man emerges from behind the curtain pulling two chains into the room. Attached to the chains, my children stumble forward. Scratched and bruised, their eyes are brimming with pain. Nevertheless, it all falls away when they look up at me.

"Mommy!" They yell as they run to me.

The chains at their throats catch them before they reach me.

I look at the man at the table. "I'm taking them."

He smiles. "You may only have them for the right price."

"I have water and food."

"What good are food and water if hunger and thirst are never satisfied?"

"I have salt, a cross, and a stake."

"What for?"

"For protection from the demons."

The madman laughs hard. He clutches his stomach. His servant also belts out a scratchy laugh.

"To protect you from demons?" The madman's voice is filled with mirth. "Did you not notice that there aren't any demons in Hell? All of the demons are on Earth. Humans are the only ones in Hell." He sips his wine and collects himself. "Besides, what would you do with your children if you were to take them from me? You're all still stuck in Hell."

"We're going back to Earth."

"How?" His face drops. Hunger sits behind his eyes.

"The Devil gave me passes to get back out."

"How many?" He throws the question at me.

"Three."

Suddenly the madman is back in control. He smiles. "Perfect. You will give me one pass for your two children."

"But I need all three passes for all of us to get out."

"Do you?" He purrs. "Your name isn't Sophie, is it?"

"Why?" I ask in confusion.

"Because you have a choice to make. Take one of your children out of Hell or neither of them."

"You'll take nothing else?"

"No." He smirks.

I pause to think.

"Take the offer." He interrupts the brief silence. "You got into Hell the first time. Get one to safety and then come back for the other."

I sigh. I don't see a way around it. I can't fight the two men. I also can't leave my children with him.

"Fine."

The madman motions for the servant to unchain my children. They run into my arms and bury their faces into my chest. I kiss the tops of their heads, feeling their soft hair against my face.

I look up and the madman is inches from my face.

"The pass?" He holds out his hand.

I give him one of our passes. He thanks me before heading behind the curtain with his servant.

"Come, let's go." I say to my children.

I lead my children back through the multiple levels of Hell. Our hands are interlocked. I keep my children far away from each person we pass. I carry them when they are tired. When they are thirsty, I give them water. When they complain of hunger, I hand them food from my pack. This time, the walk is too short. We make it to the gate in no time at all.

I can't stop the tears from falling. I pull my children close. I hug them tighter than ever before. I hunch down to their face level.

"We all can't go back through the gate."

My children don't understand. Confusion clouds their faces.

I look my son in the eyes. "You remember where Aunty Hannah lives, right?"

He nods.

"Good." I place a pass into his hands. "Mommy needs you to take your sister to Aunty Hannah's house. Can you do that?"

He nods. "What about you Mommy?"

"I'll join you later. Don't worry about me. Worry about your sister."

"Okay," he agrees.

I put the second pass into my daughter's hands. I pull my children together. "Hold hands now." I command.

My children comply. I kiss their heads one last time before I send them towards the gate. The gate swings open to let them pass and it swings closed behind them, leaving me in darkness. I pull the stake from my pack and wait for the madman.

Additional Story: Insomniac

I don't rob houses anymore. But when I did, it was never because I enjoyed it. I had bills to pay. Rent, grocery, and utility bills that thirty-five hours a week at my minimum wage day job didn't cover. I robbed houses because there was money in it and I had a knack for it.

On nights when I couldn't sleep, I wandered the streets. I was a ghost floating from streetlamp to streetlamp. The homes I passed became stages. I alone was privy to the shows within them. Under my gaze, intimate details were revealed. I could look at a house and determine the location of the master bedroom by the house's style and size. I could tell how many people lived in a home by the way lights and sounds traveled from room to room. From the yards alone, I could tell if the homeowners had children or dogs. There were so many details about each home's occupants in the open. You only needed to look. I noticed the homes where the doors or windows were locked. I marked the homes where the residents were careless. I noted homes where the lodger was a heavy sleeper and where the dweller would awaken at the smallest sound.

With all this information, it was easy to slip into specific homes unnoticed. I also had a strategy to keep myself from getting caught. The homes with alarms were obvious and avoided. I also only picked homes where the master bedroom was on the second floor. I tried to be quiet, but complete silence was impossible. The farther the sound had to travel to reach the sleeper's ears, the better. Before entering a home, I tapped the side. I then listened for the sound of movement or a barking dog. If there was no response, I knew it was safe to continue.

I removed my shoes outside the home and placed them in my backpack. Socks masked the sound of my movements. I gently tried the doors and windows. If I found one unlocked, I inched it open. My movements were slow to ensure they were inaudible. Once inside, I only took a few things. Game systems, games, laptops, tablets, and credit cards were placed in my backpack. I only searched the kitchen and living room. I never looked upstairs, even if I couldn't find anything. I completed my search in a few minutes before disappearing into the night.

Next, I took the credit cards to several stores. Credit cards were tricky. The cards were always reported as stolen by morning. Additionally, credit card companies would cancel the card if the transactions looked suspicious. To avoid card alerts, I bought a few groceries and a gift card at each store. I learned these rules quickly, but not without a few mistakes. Luckily, women who are small and mousy get the benefit of the doubt when the card is declined at check out.

Afterward, I performed a factory reset on the electronics. This cleared personal information from the device. Then, I took them to a specific reseller. You couldn't take them to a pawn shop, because the shop would get suspicious. The reseller didn't ask questions, but in exchange for his silence, he paid little for each item. I got $5 a game, $20 a game system, and $20-$50 for each laptop or tablet.

When I was robbing houses, I had no trouble buying groceries. My landlord didn't ask why rent was paid in Visa gift cards. The system worked well. I never got caught. I didn't stop because I got in trouble or because my conscience caught up with me. I stopped robbing houses because of what I saw one night.

The last house I robbed was a small two-story abode. The wooden front door sat on the left side of the home. A large, single-pane window was right of the door. The house looked depressing. Walking around the house revealed that there wasn't another door on the home. Additionally, the only other first-story window was on the back of the house. That window was small, too small to fit through. It was above the sink and offered a view into the kitchen. The first floor of the home had an open-air concept where the kitchen and living space were only separated by a bar. The front door opened up to the living room and a set of stairs were flush with the wall. Judging by the home's small size, the master bedroom and bathroom must be upstairs.

I walked around the home until I was back at the front. If I couldn't get in via the front door or adjacent window, I would have to try another home. Taking off my shoes, I placed them in my backpack. I twisted the doorknob, but it was locked. Next, I moved to the window. I pushed the window upwards and it slid open a few centimeters. Perfect. Slipping my fingers under the pane, I inched the window up. When it was open, I placed my leg through the hole. My foot landed on a couch cushion. I contorted my body through the opening before gently closing the window. The light from the moon poured through the window, but most of the space lay in shadow. Standing still for a few moments, I let my eyes adjust to the dark.

Each step I took into the home was timid. I tested the floor beneath each footfall for the sounds of creaking or settling. I unlocked the front door to make a quick escape if necessary. Then, I began my work. I checked the TV stand for any game systems or games. There were only speakers and the TV. I never took TVs because they were too large to carry. I searched the side tables and coffee table for a laptop or tablet. I could only find a remote and some paperback books and a few magazines. There wasn't enough light to make out the covers.

Unfettered, I headed to the kitchen. The countertops were empty except for a few appliances. I started checking the drawers. It was just junk. I sighed, but I made out a faint sound above my exhale. There was a footfall above me. My heart dropped. I looked towards the door, but footsteps were coming down the stairs. I wouldn't make it in time. Frantically, I looked around the kitchen. I would never make it out the kitchen window. But in the darkness, I made out a door. Pulling it open, I found a pantry. It would do. I wedged myself inside and drew it almost shut. I left an opening wide enough to see out. From the pantry, I could see into the kitchen and living room.

A man emerged from the stairs. He was naked, except for his underwear. The moonlight shone through the window and reflected off his pale skin. He was thin. His flesh was pulled tight across his bones. Dark hair fell across a blank face. He moved silently, but a small cat mewed behind him.

The man picked up a remote and pressed a few buttons. Music began playing in the living room. The song sounded like it belonged in a children's show. It was repetitive and grossly cheery. The lyrics were nonsense. I made out 'My name is' and nothing else.

Through the dark, I saw the man begin dancing. Or something that might have been called dancing. In time with the beat, he moved one body part at a time. The rest of his body was eerily still. First, his knees bent, then his shoulders, and elbows. It reminded me of an animatronic.

The song ended, but he restarted it. Moving through the same robotic dance, his face remained emotionless. What was I watching? I was intruding on a private moment, but I couldn't help but wonder why he was dancing. I also couldn't sleep well at night, but I never felt the need to do a weird dance to children's music in my underwear. Was he even awake or was he sleepwalking?

The song ended a second time, but he restarted it again. Bending knees, shrugging shoulders, and shifting elbows, he continued his strange pattern. How long could this go on? I wanted to leave. He only needed to go upstairs for a few minutes and I could run out the door. The song ended a third time and he turned it off. My sigh of relief was nearly audible.

The cat mewed again from the shadowy corner. In a single swoop, the man swung the cat up from the floor. He cradled the cat in his arms. Rocking the cat for a few moments, they both seemed calmer. The man brought the cat to his face and licked the cat's head. I gagged at the sight. I had to hold my hand over my mouth to prevent the sound from reaching the man. He licked the cat again as if he was a feline himself. A pale, hairless biped feline in small white underwear. Each lick was slow and long. The cat sat patiently and offered no resistance. I cringed from the pantry. I wanted to leave, but the man blocked my only exit. The cat mewed a final time and the man placed the cat down.

The man's gaze moved to the kitchen. I froze. Did he hear me? He walked up to a cabinet and opened it. I relaxed the tension that built up while he walked to the kitchen. Taking a plate from the cabinet, the man examined it. Without reason, he threw it on the floor. It shattered with a loud crash. He grabbed another plate and smashed it. With one hand he removed a dish and tossed it to the floor. His other hand grabbed the next dish to repeat the process. He was destroying his plates and bowls at a rapid pace. I didn't understand what was wrong with this man. Soon the cabinet was empty. The man sat down on the floor. Taking a dish shard, he pressed it against the skin of his arm. A thin dark line cut across his pale skin. The blood dripped down his arm. The wound was shallow, but he moved to make another cut.

My heart was in my throat. Tears sat in the corners of my eyes. Unbeknownst to my discomfort, the man continued cutting himself.I couldn't take this anymore. I threw the pantry door open. Startled, the man stood up. I plowed past him towards the front door. The man fell into the pile of broken dishware, but I didn't care. I ran out of the house. I didn't stop moving until I was in my home and the deadbolt was locked behind me.

So, I don't rob houses anymore. After a difficult few weeks, I found a job working overnight as a desk clerk for a hotel. The pay was stable and I was awake most nights anyway. I searched the papers for any mention of a suspicious death or home invasion. There was nothing. The man must not have been hurt too badly by his fall. I even checked on him several weeks later. One morning I hid down the street and waited for him to leave for work. The man who left the home looked well-adjusted and normal. He was someone who I would see on the street and immediately forget. He looked nothing like the creature from that night. I wonder what he thought of me. After all, I was the monster that barged out of his pantry and threw him onto the shards. Of the two of us, whose nightmare were we in that night?

Additional Story: The Lighthouse of Madness

"The lighthouse of madness has been lit. A cry for help in this world of shit."

"What the fuck does that mean?" I ask Colin in vain.

We found Colin outside the burnt rubble of an apartment building a few weeks back. He was wandering the parking lot, blackened with ash. We thought he was dead, but then he spoke. In rhyme. The dead don't do that.

"Smoke signals so wide that all can see. Something so brash only the mad would be."

I sigh. "Would *do*. Would *be* doesn't make sense. You can't ignore grammatical rules to make the rhyme work."

What on earth happened to Colin that led him to speak in verse? We all have been through shit. The dead rose from their graves. It is literally the end of times,but everyone else is talking normally. Except for Colin. And the zombies, who just moan and groan.

"Wait, Colin is right," Sarah stands and points across the horizon. Gray smoke stands out across the blue sky.

"Is that a fire?"

"It must be massive," Sarah walks around the RV.

"Eric, there is a fire up ahead!" She shouts.

Eric sticks his head out of the RV. "A fire? Man made?"

Sarah shakes her head. "I don't know."

"Well, we found Colin by following the smoke. Maybe we can find him a mad girlfriend this time?" I tease.

Eric frowns. The situation is too serious for jokes. But, everything has been too serious for jokes.

"A fire so large and fierce and bright. Indicates willpower and determination and fight."

"Colin is right. We need to go check it out," Eric, ever the leader, pronounces to his subjects. "Anna and Sarah, clean up the campsite. Colin, tell Daniel it is time to go. And hurry."

We spring into action. To survive this long during the zombie apocalypse, we have to be fast. In the span of a few minutes, everything is packed, we are buckled in our seats, and Eric is shifting into drive. Outside the window of our RV, we pass crashed cars, decaying bodies, and broken homes. The standard views of our world now.

"What city is this?"

"Chapel Hill," Sarah answers.

"The college town?" Daniel asks.

Sarah nods.

"A center of learning and knowledge," Colin pauses.

He is struggling to find a rhyme for knowledge. I've never seen him miss a verse before, but I know he will one day.

"A prestigious university college," Colin finishes.

Does that really count? One day he will mess up and maybe then he'll realize how weird this all is. Maybe.

As we approach downtown, the smoke thickens. A tower of flame appears above us.

"Is it safe to be this close?" I ask Sarah. Sarah seems to know everything.

"Eric, maybe we should stop here. We don't have anything to fight those flames," Sarah shouts to the front.

The RV rolls to a stop. Eric puts the RV into park and turns to us. "The fire is still active. Let head back a bit."

Eric turns back around, but before he gets the RV into drive, Colin is gone. He unbuckles himself and darts out the door before anyone can stop him.

"Colin!" Eric shouts, but it is no use. Colin is running into the smoke.

"Maybe Colin was a fire fighter and his natural instincts are kicking in."

Daniel narrows his eyes at me. "Grow up Anna."

I stare back and frown. "I'm fucking fourteen Daniel. How grown up should I be?"

"Stop it you two!" Sarah waves her hands between us. "We can't leave Colin here."

"No, we can't," Eric agrees. "I'll drive ahead slowly. You three look for Colin."

I press my face to the glass. Where did that idiot go? The RV plows ahead at a snail's pace.

"I see him!" Daniel shouts.

Through the smoke, Colin runs toward us. Over his shoulders, he has slung a body. Daniel throws the RV door open and Colin bolts inside, slinging the body on the floor.

"Are they still alive?" Eric peers over our shoulders.

Ash flutters over the body's face. I lean closer, even as Sarah pulls me back. The body is moaning. No, she is speaking. I put my ear to her mouth.

"Knock . . . knock," she labors.

I snap up. "She is alive, but maybe crazy."

"Anna!" Sarah scolds.

"What? She is starting a knock-knock joke, but where is the punch-line?"

Eric stands. "I'm driving out of here. Sarah, Daniel, and Anna clean her up. And make sure she doesn't turn. We'll wait outside the town until the fire clears."

"The lighthouse of madness brings a gift. The keeper herself, set adrift."

"Good one Colin," I retort as we lift his *gift* to the bed in the back of the RV. Eric's kingdom grows to five: Colin, Sarah, Daniel, the mad girl, and me.

www.ingramcontent.com/pod-product-compliance
Lightning Source LLC
Chambersburg PA
CBHW071233170626
46809CB00008BA/3040